"I'll do whatever it takes to keep you safe.

"Want me to take a bullet for you to prove it?" Jack didn't wink, but he might as well have because he was obviously trying to lighten up things. Trying to bring her back down and ease some of the raw adrenaline. It was working, sort of, since it was something he'd said to her in jest when they were lovers. A way of letting her know that he cared that much for her.

"No." There was a lot more emotion in her voice than Caroline wanted, and she was staring at him.

Thinking.

Remembering.

Yes, definitely remembering.

Despite everything she'd been through—or maybe because of it—Caroline wanted to step right into his arms. Those strong arms with their corded muscles. She wanted to feel the heat, and the comfort, that she'd gotten there before. Jack had tugged and pulled at her in a way that no man ever had before.

HIS BRAND OF JUSTICE

USA TODAY Bestselling Author

DELORES FOSSEN

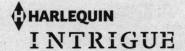

HARLEQUIN
INTRIGUE

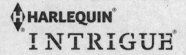

HARLEQUIN®
INTRIGUE®

Recycling programs for this product may not exist in your area.

ISBN-13: 978-1-335-13598-8

His Brand of Justice

Copyright © 2020 by Delores Fossen

This edition published by arrangement with Harlequin Books S.A.

For questions and comments about the quality of this book, please contact us at CustomerService@Harlequin.com.

Harlequin Enterprises ULC
22 Adelaide St. West, 40th Floor
Toronto, Ontario M5H 4E3, Canada
www.Harlequin.com

Printed in U.S.A.

Delores Fossen, a *USA TODAY* bestselling author, has written over one hundred novels, with millions of copies of her books in print worldwide. She's received a Booksellers' Best Award and an RT Reviewers' Choice Best Book Award. She was also a finalist for a prestigious RITA® Award. You can contact the author through her website at www.deloresfossen.com.

Books by Delores Fossen

Visit the Author Profile page at Harlequin.com.

CAST OF CHARACTERS

Jack Slater—This tough cowboy marshal must protect his old flame even though she suspects the person trying to kill her is one of his fellow lawmen.

Caroline Moser—A former profiler who has a killer after her, and the only man she can trust is someone who could crush her heart.

Lily Terrell—The San Antonio socialite who appears to be a do-gooder, but she might be using her money to cover her criminal activities.

Marshal Lee Zeller—Is he hiding behind his badge so he can locate Caroline and kill her because he thinks she can link him to a murder?

Kingston Morris—Rich and spoiled, he's become a serial killer groupie, and he might have an old bone to pick with Caroline.

Grace Wainwright—A computer hacker who's possibly sheltering the identity of a killer, or she could be in hiding because she's in fear for her own life.

Chapter One

The moment Marshal Jack Slater brought his truck to a stop in front of the small country house, he drew his gun, threw open the door and raced up the porch steps. He'd already glanced around the road and the sprawling yard to see if there was any immediate danger. If there was, he hadn't spotted anything.

That didn't mean, though, that there wasn't a threat.

And that was why Jack had gotten here as fast as he could, once he'd received the call from the live-in nurse, Lucille Booker. From the instant he'd heard Lucille say "Marshal Slater, there might be a problem" in a breathy voice, Jack had known there was no *might* to it. There was trouble. Lucille had been at this job for three months, and never once had he heard that kind of concern in her voice. No, not just concern.

Fear.

Jack didn't knock. Instead, he flipped up the

top of what appeared to be an ordinary doorbell to reveal a panel for the security system beneath it. He punched in the code, which would alert the two women inside that it was him. Only when he heard the clicks that let him know the alarms and locks had been temporarily disarmed did he open the door.

Lucille was there in the foyer, and she had a gun in the white-knuckle grip of her right hand. A gun that Jack had issued to her after making sure that she knew how to use it.

There was no blood on her, thank God. No signs of any injury, and the room showed no indications of a struggle. Everything in the house was neat and tidy, as it usually was.

Lucille was what no one would call petite— another reason Jack had wanted her for this job. Her beefy build, no-fuss choppy brown hair and sharply angled face all gave her the appearance of a woman who knew how to take care of herself. And it was true. In addition to being a nurse with twenty years of experience, Lucille had been an instructor of self-defense classes for women.

"What happened?" Jack asked as he reset the security system. "Where's Caroline?"

An answer to that second question wasn't necessary, though, because he soon saw the blonde in the kitchen. Caroline Moser. Jack cursed, because she was standing there with a butcher knife.

Unlike Lucille, there was nothing beefy about Caroline. She was lean and tall, and the loose pale blue cotton dress she was wearing didn't disguise her willowy body. She had an angel's face, he'd always thought. Like some painting on a museum wall. Once, before things had gone to hell in a handbasket, there'd been a lot of toughness and street smarts beneath those soft, delicate features.

No toughness now, though.

She was way too pale, and she looked way too fragile.

"When Caroline and I were clearing up after lunch, I saw a man," Lucille explained. "A stranger. He was by the pond."

Not good. No one should have been within a quarter of a mile of this place, since it wasn't anywhere on the beaten path. Of course, Jack could say that about lots of properties in the county, which was mainly made up of ranches, farms and small towns. Like Longview Ridge, the place where Jack had been born and raised and where he still lived. This safe house was only about fifteen miles from there—and from him. But it was still far enough away that someone shouldn't have just strolled by here.

"You saw this man, too?" he asked Caroline.

"Just a glimpse." There was plenty of worry and fear in her voice, but there was something else in her jewel-green eyes.

Suspicion.

Jack knew that particular reaction was for him.

She didn't trust him, not completely, anyway, and he'd seen that look plenty of times over the past three months since he'd become her handler in WITSEC. Before that, when she had known who he was, there'd been other emotions...ones that he wished he couldn't remember, either.

Jack wasn't sure why the doubt was there now. Or all the other times he'd visited her here in this safe house over the past weeks. Her doctors had said it was because of the trauma from her injuries and her amnesia. It was hard for her to trust anyone, they'd said, when there were way too many blanks in her mind.

Still, it cut him to the bone.

Of course, there were plenty other things that he should be thinking about right now, things that didn't involve whether she trusted him or not, and Jack went to the kitchen window. That vantage point would give him a good view of not only the pond but also the small barn and pasture.

Other than the two horses that Jack had personally delivered to the place, nothing and no one was out there. However, since Lucille wasn't easily spooked, she must have seen someone.

"You didn't recognize the man?" Jack pressed, glancing back at Lucille.

The nurse shook her head. She put away her gun in the slide holster at the back of her scrubs. "But he had dark hair and was wearing jeans and a black T-shirt. He darted behind the big oak tree when he spotted me."

Darting definitely wasn't a good sign, but Jack was holding out hope that this was just someone who'd strayed onto the property, only to realize that he was trespassing. Too bad the twisting feeling in his gut let him know that wasn't the case.

"I called you right away, just as you told me to do," Lucille added. "And I made sure Caroline stayed away from the windows." Again, that was as Jack had instructed.

Jack made a sound of approval, and while continuing to volley his attention out the window, he reached out to take the knife from Caroline. Her hand went stiff when his fingers brushed over hers. Actually, every part of her seemed to stiffen as her gaze collided with his. Her intense stare held a few long moments before she finally let go of the knife.

"Sorry, Marshal Slater," she muttered. "I'm a little spooked."

Marshal Slater. It wasn't a surprise that she called him that. In fact, it was the only thing Caroline had called him since she'd turned up in Longview Ridge three months ago with that head injury and the amnesia. She said his name with the same edgy suspicion that was in her eyes.

Before the memory loss, she had called him Jack. And there'd sure as hell been no suspicion then. Only the heat from the scalding hot fire that he no longer saw or felt in any part of her.

I love you, Jack.

Those were the last words Caroline had said to him before she was taken hostage, before this nightmare had begun. Words she'd said when they thought it would be an ordinary, short goodbye. When Jack had thought there'd be plenty of other times for him to say *I love you* right back—and that was why he hadn't said it to her then. Now he might never get the chance.

He was a stranger to her now. He was *Marshal Slater*.

Jack tried not to let that eat away at him, especially since Lucille had insisted on calling him by his title and surname, too. But in Lucille's case, it just sounded as if she'd wanted to remind herself that he was there to protect Caroline and her. Which he was.

"You think it was a false alarm?" Lucille asked, joining him at the window.

Jack lifted his shoulder. "The sensors weren't tripped."

If they had been, Jack would have gotten the alert on his phone. Of course, the guy would have had to get closer to the house for that to happen, since the sensors were arranged around the perimeter of the yard and on the dirt road that led to the house.

There were also some cameras, and Jack fired off a text to his partner, Marshal Teagan Randolph. He asked her to cull out the video feed from all the cameras for the past hour and send it to him ASAP.

"I'll wait around for a while and keep watch," he assured Lucille and Caroline when he was done with the text.

A while was going to mean staying for the night. Or longer. He didn't intend to take any risks with Caroline, because somewhere in those lost memories in her head was a piece of information he needed as much as the next breath he took.

She knew who'd murdered his father.

The images came. They always did whenever he thought of his dad, Sheriff Buck Slater. Buck had been the law in Longview Ridge, but that had ended one night in a hail of bullets and blood when someone had gunned him down. Caroline was the only person alive who could tell him what'd happened.

Other than the killer, of course.

And Jack suspected he wouldn't be getting any answers from him or her on that. Especially since he had a mile-long suspect list that he hadn't managed to whittle down much since his father's murder a little over a year ago.

He was betting Caroline was eager to uncover those memories, too. Well, maybe she was. She had to want to know what'd happened not just to his father but also to her. She would want to know how she got that head injury. But the doctors had said the amnesia could be a way of protecting herself from a nightmare that was too traumatic for her to face. Still, Jack had to hold on to hope that one day she would push the trauma aside and help him catch a killer.

"I'll make a fresh pot of coffee," Lucille volunteered, and she got busy doing that after she gave Caroline the once-over.

It was the kind of quick exam a nurse would take of her patient, probably to make sure Caroline wasn't on the verge of a panic attack. Jack hadn't witnessed one of the attacks, but he'd heard from Lucille and then Caroline's doctors that she'd had several in the three months that she'd been in WITSEC. It was the reason the

US Marshals—and Jack himself—had wanted a nurse to be with her. Normally, when someone was placed in WITSEC, that didn't happen. The person merely started a new life with a new identity and no past.

But nothing about this situation was normal.

Jack had also had to convince his agency that this wouldn't be a conflict of interest for him, that he could do his job as Caroline's handler despite their prior personal relationship. And that it would be all right for him to place her in the local area where he could keep a close eye on her. Maybe some of his fellow marshals did know of his personal interest in the case. But none had doubted that he would do whatever it took to make sure Caroline was not only safe but that she also made a full recovery. Emphasis on the *full*.

When Lucille had moved from the kitchen window, Caroline had came closer to him. But not too close. She always gave him a wide berth, making sure they didn't accidentally bump into each other. Maybe that's why his merely touching her hand earlier had caused every muscle in her body to turn to iron.

"You think that man by the pond came here to kill me?" she asked.

If he hadn't thought that was possible, she wouldn't need to be in WITSEC. But the truth was, he just didn't know. Maybe there was no killer after Caroline, but he wasn't willing to take that chance. Because if there was someone after her, it would likely be the same person who'd murdered his father. The person could want to silence her permanently so she could never reveal his or her identity.

"We don't know who we're dealing with," he settled for saying. He usually gave her a variation of that whenever the subject of her safety came up. Which was often. No need to alarm her and spur one of those panic attacks by spelling out worst-case scenarios. "Was there anything about this man you recognized?"

"No. Like I said, I only got a glimpse." Caroline didn't hesitate, but she did huff. "Has my location been compromised? Will I have to move to another safe house?"

Possibly, but Jack decided to put a softer spin on that. "Let's just wait and see. I'm not going to let anything happen to you." He looked at her as the last of those words were leaving his mouth, and for just a split second he saw something more than distrust on her face.

Anger, maybe?

But it was gone as quickly as it had come.

"I don't know who killed your father," she insisted. The riled expression might be gone, but there was a tinge of agitation in her voice.

Jack glanced at Lucille to see if she had an explanation for this change in Caroline's attitude, and the nurse's mouth tightened a little. "Caroline found some articles on the internet."

Well, hell. That definitely explained it. There were plenty of sites that had gobs of sordid details about his father's shooting. About Deputy Dusty Walters, who'd also died that night, too. And Caroline's name came up often on those sites. Not in a good way, either. The press had had a field day with her because she'd disappeared. There'd been plenty of speculation that had gone along with questions about where she was and what'd happened to her.

Not many people knew the answer to that.

WITSEC had taken care of shielding her identity so that now she lived and worked in this house. In fact, work was the reason she had a laptop in the first place. The Justice Department had created a job for her where she was reviewing witness testimony in cases where no charges had been filed. It was one step above busy work, but obviously it hadn't kept her busy enough.

"Yes, the filters are still on the computer," Lucille assured him.

"I figured out how to get around them," Caroline quickly confessed. "And no, it wasn't something I remembered how to do. I just kept plugging away until I found a web page that the filter didn't catch."

Jack added another "hell." He'd need to tell the doctors about this so they could deal with it during her weekly therapy session. A session that would, ironically, be done online, since Jack had wanted to limit Caroline's visits into San Antonio along with also limiting the number of people who knew the location of the safe house. And he'd managed to do that by limiting that info to his partner, Lucille and his three brothers, who were all lawmen. Jack had wanted them to know in case they needed to make a quick response.

However, even with all the precautions they'd taken, Jack knew that the safe house information could be breached. Their computer filters were more elaborate than the ones on the laptop here, but someone determined to find Caroline could still get around them. A killer definitely fell into the "someone determined" category.

Caroline groaned softly and pushed her shoulder-length blond hair from her face. "I used to have a life. I've read about it," she added in a grumble. "I came from almost nothing. My prostitute mother was killed by a drug dealer when I was eight, and I ended up in foster care." She looked ready to tack on more to that recap of her childhood, but then she stopped, paused.

"I got through all of that to get a job working for one of the top criminal profiling experts."

Jack nodded. Yep, all of that was true. She'd had a life, all right, and even though she was alive, she might never get that life back. Would certainly never undo the fallout to her reputation because of the work she'd done with that top expert.

What Caroline hadn't just mentioned in the rundown of her life was her police record. A sealed juvie rap sheet that she wouldn't have been able to access without the prime hacking skills that she'd had before she lost her memory.

This woman with the angel face and almost fragile-looking body had been arrested when she was fifteen for hacking into multiple state records to find the dealer who'd killed her mother. Caroline had then stolen a car, tracked down the man and managed to bash him in the gut with a baseball bat before calling the cops to come and get him. The cops had gone easy on her because of the extenuating circumstances, but she'd still spent some time in juvie lockup.

"I saw a picture of Eric Lang," Caroline went on. She groaned again. "I suppose you know all there is to know about him." But she waved that off. "Of course, you do. You're a marshal. You're Sheriff Buck Slater's son."

Jack stayed quiet, but he knew Eric all right.

Eric had been the research assistant for Caroline and her boss/friend Gemma Hanson at the college where the three of them had been working on a new computer program for profiling serial killers. The irony was that Eric himself had been a serial killer, and neither Gemma nor Caroline had picked up on it. Eric had hidden it from the women. From everyone. Then, Eric had nearly killed both Caroline and Gemma when he'd taken them hostage. That was what had sent Jack's father to an abandoned hotel, where he'd been killed.

Gemma had managed to escape that night. Caroline hadn't. Eric had taken her and disappeared into the darkness with her. No one, not even Caroline, was certain what had happened after that, but she'd shown up in Longview Ridge a year later. Because of her amnesia, though, she hadn't been able to tell them what'd happened to her.

"Eric is dead," Jack reminded her. "He was shot and killed three months ago, shortly after you came back to Longview Ridge."

Of course, he'd already told her that, and she had almost certainly read about it in those internet articles, but Jack wanted to spell it out for her that she didn't have to be afraid of Eric. He couldn't come after her again.

"Was I stupid?" she blurted out. Man, the

anger had returned with a vengeance, not just in her tone but in her expression. "Was that why I couldn't see a serial killer was working right next to me?"

Jack hated to see her beating herself up like this. "You definitely weren't stupid. I met Eric, too, and I didn't make him for a killer. A lot of people didn't."

That didn't seem to appease her one bit. Her forehead still stayed bunched up, making the scar there even more obvious. A scar that she'd gotten during her captivity. Possibly from Eric, when he'd clubbed her on the head that night she was taken hostage. Of course, until Caroline got back her memory, she wouldn't be able to confirm if that was what had actually happened.

"And what about *us*?" Caroline threw out there.

Lucille's gaze fired to Caroline, then him. Jack didn't know what to make of the question, either. In the past three months, Caroline hadn't asked about them as a couple, but that was because Jack had never stayed around for an actual conversation. He visited twice a week, to check if Caroline's memory had returned. And once Lucille and Caroline assured him that it hadn't, he always left.

Just as Lucille did now.

The nurse must have thought they needed

some privacy, because she mumbled something about needing to get something from her bedroom and walked out. Jack hadn't even been sure that Lucille knew Caroline and he had once been lovers.

Had been in love, he mentally corrected.

Jack hadn't talked about that with Lucille or anyone else, for that matter. Still, maybe Lucille had picked up on something or had been doing her own reading about Caroline. That would only be natural, he supposed, since Lucille and Caroline lived under the same roof, and Lucille was partly responsible for Caroline's safety.

"There was something about *us* in the articles you read?" Jack countered.

Best not to blurt out any details that Caroline didn't know or hadn't remembered. That was what the doctors had told him to do anyway. Keep the interaction between them to a minimum so there'd be no risk of planting memories in her head. That way, when she did recall something, it would be because it was a genuine memory. It was another reason he'd need to let her doctors know about this conversation.

When Caroline didn't answer, he looked at her. He saw maybe a flicker of recognition, or something, before she turned away. As she'd done earlier, she waved that off.

Jack would have pressed her for more info, pushing just a little, but his phone dinged, and he saw the file his partner, Teagan, had sent. Lucille must have heard the sound, too, because she hurried back into the kitchen.

"Any problem?" Lucille asked.

"Video from the security cameras." He motioned for her to come closer so she could take a look. When Caroline moved in, too, Jack had to consider which would upset her more: if she saw a would-be killer or if he kept her from seeing one.

He decided to let her watch.

It put them in close contact, with Lucille on one side of him and Caroline on the other. Caroline still didn't touch him, even though her arm was less than an inch from his.

Jack sped up the feed, going through minutes of what the cameras had recorded. Minutes of nothing.

And then there was something.

He slowed down the speed and then paused it when the man came into view. The guy was just as Lucille had described him—dark hair and jeans, and he was indeed by the pond. Too bad the guy was turned away from the camera so that only the side of his face was visible.

The man didn't have a drawn weapon, but Jack didn't like the way he was just standing there. If this was someone who'd just wandered onto the property, he should have been firing glances all around. Or leaving.

Jack touched the screen, moving it frame by frame until he finally got a shot he wanted. The guy turned to face the camera. Jack paused it again, enlarging it so he could run it through facial recognition software.

Caroline gasped. "Oh, God. Jack, I know him."

Shaking her head, she stepped back and pressed her fingers to her mouth. But only for a moment. Caroline's eyes widened when she saw that she'd gotten his complete attention. He could also see that she quickly tried to shut back down to that flat expression she'd worn for the past three months. But it was too late for that.

For that mask.

Because Jack had seen the recognition in her eyes. Better yet, he'd heard it in her voice.

Jack.

"You remembered something?" Lucille quickly asked, maybe not picking up on the sudden slash of tension between her patient and Jack. "Do you really know who that man is?"

Caroline didn't even look at the nurse. She kept her gaze fastened on Jack. Recognition, definitely. And some defiance. She hiked up her chin, and her mouth went into a flat line.

"Yes, I know that man," Caroline said, her stare drilling into Jack. "And I know *you*."

Chapter Two

Caroline's heart had gone to her knees at the exact moment she'd said Jack's name. Mercy, what had she done?

She wanted to take back the last handful of seconds, wanted to fix her expression so that Jack wouldn't see right through her. But she couldn't. The lid was off Pandora's box, and it wasn't going back on. And if that wasn't bad enough, now she had that face on the security video to worry about.

Caroline swallowed hard and looked at Lucille, who immediately took hold of her arm. "You need to sit down," Lucille instructed. "You look like you're about to pass out." She tried to lead Caroline back into the living room, but she held her ground. "Did your memory really come back?" Lucille asked.

"Yes," Caroline managed to say.

Lucille let out a huge breath of relief. Of course, the nurse didn't know how dangerous the man she'd recognized was. She also didn't know something Jack had already figured out.

That she'd regained her memory days ago.

As if celebrating and relieved by the progress, Lucille hugged her. "I'll need to call your doctor. Maybe we can drive out to see him?"

Even though Caroline liked her doctors and she'd had no trouble on the previous trips to San Antonio for her exams, she definitely didn't want a doctor right now.

"No. Could you give me a moment alone with Marshal Slater?" Caroline asked. It probably seemed petty or insulting to Jack that she'd call him by his surname now, but saying *Jack* seemed too, well, intimate.

Considering all the other intimate things they'd done, it would be so easy to slip back into that. After all, she had only told one man that she loved him, and it was the same man who was now glaring at her.

Lucille continued to give her a long, concerned look. "Should I get your meds?"

"No," Caroline repeated. "I'm not going to have a panic attack." She thought that was true, anyway, and even if it wasn't, she couldn't deal with the haze that the meds created in her mind. "I just need a moment with Marshal Slater. It's…personal."

"Oh." Lucille seemed relieved, which meant

that maybe she knew or had guessed that Jack and Caroline had once been involved.

Jack knew it too, of course. There was nothing wrong with his memory. Or his glare. He stood there, all lanky and lean, looking more cop than cowboy now—though he was both. He'd come from a long line of Texas cowboys, and it fit him as well as his jeans and his ice-blue shirt.

No ice in his eyes, though. There was so much fire and heat in the depths of all that gray. The color of a dangerous storm cloud ready to shoot some lightning bolts her way. His hair was even darker than that. Midnight black. And right now his clothes, his expression and everything else about him made him seem more than a little dangerous.

Caroline waited until Lucille was out of the room before she said anything else. She turned to Jack, and she answered his question before he could even ask it. "Three days ago. That's when I regained my memory."

Muscles stirred in his jaw, and she doubted his eyes could narrow even more. "Why the hell didn't you tell me?" he asked through clenched teeth.

Oh, he was so not going to like this, and worse, she wasn't going to have time to smooth it over. No time to try to make him understand.

"I don't know who killed your father. That's the truth."

"And I'm just to believe that after you've lied to me for three days, or longer?" Jack snarled.

Good point, and Caroline conceded that with a weary sound of agreement. It hadn't been longer, but she doubted she could convince him of that.

"The night Eric Lang kidnapped me, he did injure me," Caroline continued. "He bashed me on the head with his gun." She idly rubbed the scar on her forehead that she'd gotten from that attack. "And when that wasn't enough to render me unconscious, he pumped me full of drugs. Then he hid me and Gemma in one of the rooms of the abandoned hotel, Serenity Inn."

No need for her to get into too many specifics on the location. Jack had almost certainly searched every inch of that old hotel and gone over all the details of the investigation that followed. He knew that Eric had indeed managed to escape with her, and Jack had likely found her blood or some other evidence in that crumbling, smothering room that had once been part of a Victorian mansion.

"Eric didn't kill your father," she went on. "Eric was with me, holding a gun to my bleeding head when I heard the shots. And yes, I know it was the shots that killed your dad, because I also heard Gemma scream. I could hear the chaos that followed." She had to pause and gather her breath. With her breath, though, came the images.

Mercy, the images.

Caroline had to try to rein all of that in. If she had a panic attack, Lucille would force her into taking those meds, and that couldn't happen. She needed to finish what she had to say.

"Eric got away with me," Caroline went on several moments later while Jack stood there and drilled holes in her with his intense stare. "By then, I was barely conscious, but he talked to someone on the phone. A cop or some kind of lawman. And that person helped him escape. I know the caller was in law enforcement because there was a police radio in the background."

She didn't expect Jack to buy that, and even if he did, it still wouldn't justify her withholding the information that she'd regained her memory or the fact that she hadn't trusted him enough to tell him.

"Before I got my memory fully back, before I remembered *us*, I thought the person talking to Eric that night was you," she said. That didn't come out right, so she shook her head. "Or rather, someone you knew, because the other words I heard were 'Longview Ridge Sheriff's Office.' I heard dispatch codes. I thought it could be someone you wouldn't believe would help a serial killer, and that your disbelief would allow him to get to me or someone else."

Now he cursed, and those jaw muscles went to war with each other. "I'm not dirty, and I don't know any marshal or cop who is. I sure as hell wouldn't have helped Eric."

"Maybe not. But someone with a badge did. And I decided that if I wanted to stay alive, I couldn't trust you, the other marshals or anyone in your family."

He opened his mouth as if to blast her with verbal fire, but then he stopped, and it looked as if he'd done some reining in of his emotions, as well. "Yet you let me put you here. You let me come here to visit you."

She lifted her shoulder, tapped her head. "I didn't know, not when I came here. Three days ago, when the memories came, I decided I was safe as long as you and everyone connected to you thought I wasn't a threat. Or as long as you believed that I could eventually tell you who killed your father." Caroline took his phone. "But he's a threat. I don't have to guess about that."

Jack's glare got even worse, and she could tell the last thing he wanted to do was switch subjects. But he was also a lawman, and he'd seen the way she'd reacted to the man. Of course, maybe he thought she had faked that fear, too.

She hadn't.

"His name is Kingston Morris," she continued when Jack didn't say anything else. "And he was friends with Eric. The fact that he's here means he knows where I am and that he could have come here to kill me. Maybe to tidy up loose ends for his old friend."

"Kingston Morris," he repeated, not just once but several times as if testing to see if it rang any bells. "His name didn't come up in the investigation."

"It wouldn't have. I only remember Kingston coming in one time to the office where Eric and I worked."

"The office at the college." There was plenty of skepticism in his voice. "And yet you remembered him after just one meeting."

She shrugged. "He gave me the creeps."

That was an understatement. The guy had made her skin crawl, and because Kingston had seemed to worship Eric, that was the first time Caroline had started to look at Eric in a different light. That was the beginning of her seeing the monster crouched just below the facade he put on as a research assistant. Too bad she hadn't seen it a whole lot sooner. If she had, Jack's dad might be alive. Many others, too.

"If Eric and he were friends, Kingston's name should have come up," Jack concluded.

"Eric had erased all of his contacts. Or rather, he only left contacts and info that he didn't mind being discovered. He just used burner phones for getting in touch with anyone who was important to him."

"And this Kingston was important?" Jack asked while he typed something on his phone. She then heard the swooshes of outgoing texts. Maybe he was reaching out to his marshal friends to do a quick background check on Kingston. She hoped he hadn't mentioned that she'd regained her memory.

She nodded in reply to his question. "After Eric managed to get me away from the abandoned inn, it was Kingston who helped Eric get some money. I heard their phone conversation, too, and Kingston was like a groupie. He idolized Eric, would do anything for him."

This time Jack said a single word of profanity. "And you didn't think you should give this info to someone?" He didn't wait for her to answer. "Even if you didn't trust me, you could have told the cops."

"I didn't know if I could trust them, either." She had to pause again. "And I really did have amnesia until three days ago."

He made a sound that conveyed a whole boat-load of doubt.

"I was in a hospital in Mexico," Caroline went on. "I'm not sure how I got there, but I think Eric took me across the border, and then I escaped. Or he could have left me for dead. Someone found me in a ditch and took me to the hospital. I had injuries other than just to my head. Broken bones, and I'd been beaten. There were lots of cuts and bruises on my face."

Jack couldn't dispute any of those injuries, because he had almost certainly seen the report of the medical exam that she'd been given after she returned to Longview Ridge three months ago.

"I didn't see Eric or Kingston after that, and even if I had, I might not have recognized them because of the amnesia," she admitted.

Which meant she'd be dead right now if Eric had seen her.

"After my condition improved in the Mexico hospital, they moved me to a convalescent home because I couldn't use my right hand," she explained. "Because of the head trauma, too. I stayed there until three months ago, when I started regaining pieces of my memory. I still didn't know who I was, but the name Longview Ridge kept repeating in my head."

So had Jack's name. And what she'd said to

him kept playing again and again, too. Caroline doubted he would appreciate her mentioning that now, though.

I love you, Jack.

Yes, she'd indeed told him that. After a lazy Sunday morning of sex, he'd gotten the call to go into work, and instead of saying a simple goodbye, she'd said those words aloud. They had just slipped out—as easily as the kiss he had given her only seconds earlier. She'd seen the surprise in his eyes. Maybe the "run for the hills" look. Whichever it was, he hadn't said it back to her.

Everything that came after had happened so fast that Caroline hadn't had time to think about what had been said or unsaid. Unlike the last three days. Plenty of time to think then, and she hadn't liked the conclusion. She'd been wrong to tell him she loved him, even if it had been true.

"If you thought I was such a threat, why did you stay here?" he snapped. "Why didn't you run again as soon as you remembered what had gone on?"

"I stayed so I could try to find out the truth. Like I said, I once had a life, and I want it back. I want to find out what happened that night of your father's murder, and to do that, I have to stay alive."

"And you don't believe I want you alive." It

sounded as if that disgusted him. Maybe it did. If he was clean, and she had to pray that he was, then an accusation like that would cut him to the core. But it wasn't Jack who was her biggest worry. It was any and all of the other cops and marshals who would get called into this investigation before this was over.

She opened her mouth just as something flashed through her head. Not a memory. But a really bad thought.

"Gemma," she blurted out. "Oh, God. Kingston could go after Gemma. You have to warn her."

"I already have. I sent Kellan a text to give him a heads-up that there might be a problem with Gemma's safety. *Might*," he emphasized.

Kellan was his brother, the sheriff of Longview Ridge, but he was also Gemma's fiancé. Kellan would protect her, but it twisted at Caroline's insides that she hadn't thought of contacting Gemma the moment she'd seen Kingston's face on the screen. To the best of her knowledge, Gemma hadn't actually met Kingston, but that didn't mean the man wouldn't try to go after her or anyone else who'd been connected to his now dead idol, Eric.

"Just please make sure that no one hurts her," she said.

"Funny that you'd show this much concern for

Gemma now. She's your friend and your former boss, but you lied to her, too. Lying by omission is still a lie," he insisted. "Why didn't you tell Gemma that you had regained your memory and suspected that a dirty cop could be part of this?"

"Because I knew she'd tell Kellan," Caroline readily admitted.

"Damn straight Gemma would have, and it would have been the right thing to do."

"Maybe," Caroline muttered, not convinced that it would have indeed been the *right thing*. "But when I came back to town and saw her with Kellan, I knew they were in love. Once I had my memory back, I decided that Kellan must have been a good cop or Gemma wouldn't have those feelings for him. I couldn't take the chance, though, that Kellan would say something to someone whose feelings weren't so *loving*."

"Like me," he snapped.

"No." Frustrated and flustered, Caroline shook her head. "I just couldn't risk anyone knowing—not then, anyway. I can't protect myself. Heck, I can't even shoot straight." She held up her right hand. "Too much damage from the broken bones, and I lost what muscle strength I had." She paused, pushed her hair from her face. "Lucille's been giving me self-defense training.

In another month or so, I would have been ready to tell you the truth."

He wouldn't understand the need she had to stay sheltered and protected until she could fend for herself. But then, Jack hadn't been held hostage by a serial killer.

Caroline watched the debate Jack was having with himself, and she wasn't sure if he would hold his ground and continue to stand here and press her for every detail of information in her head, or if he'd continue to be her protector.

The protector won out.

"Lucille," he called out. "Go ahead and get Caroline's and your things packed. Bring only some essentials, one bag each. I need to take you to a new location and will have someone come for the rest of your things later."

Caroline released the breath that she didn't even know she'd been holding. "Please don't bring your brothers in on this," she insisted. "Don't bring anyone else in on it. Not yet."

Jack certainly didn't agree to that, but he did head in the direction of the bedrooms. There were only two of them, hers and Lucille's, and Lucille was in Caroline's room, shoving meds and the laptop into a small duffel bag. Caroline jumped right in to help her.

Jack stood in the doorway, continuing to view the footage from the cameras. "Caroline, did you contact anyone when you did those internet searches?" he asked. Lucille left the room, probably realizing this was a good time for her to get her own things ready.

Caroline supposed that was a necessary question, but it sent a coil of anger through her. "No. I didn't have anyone I could completely trust to contact. Not even Gemma. Because, as I said, she would have told Kellan."

She left it at that, but Jack probably knew that some of those searches would have brought up pictures of Eric's victims. So many of them. Those images would haunt her, too.

"I couldn't access anything about the investigation into your father's murder." Caroline added a change of clothes to the duffel. She was about to ask him if he had any new leads, but his phone dinged before she could.

"Kingston Morris," he read aloud. Obviously, someone had run a background check for him. "Age twenty-four. Address in Dallas. No record. Trust fund baby. His folks own a successful export business." Jack held up Kingston's DMV photo for her to see.

"That's him," she verified. "But he's not in Dallas. He was by the pond about a half hour ago. Maybe you can put out an APB on him—"

"I've already done that." Jack's attention

landed on her again. "Still believe I'm trying to kill you?"

"I never believed that," she snapped. "I just thought..." But she waved that off and zipped up the duffel with a hard jerk as if it'd been the cause for the fit of temper she was feeling.

And the frustration, doubt and fear.

"I hate being afraid," she said under her breath. She hadn't meant for Jack to hear that, but judging from the way he huffed and cursed, he had. Worse, he was probably analyzing her now as the shrinks had done after she'd tracked down her mother's killer.

"Then you need to trust me." He didn't say it as a request or plea. It was an order, and he tipped his head to indicate he wanted her on the move.

Jack also drew his gun.

Her pulse hadn't exactly been at a resting pace, but the sight of the weapon jacked it up even more, as it did the hit of adrenaline. It didn't mesh well with that knot already in her stomach.

With a small suitcase gripped in her hand, Lucille joined them in the hall. "How close are you parked to the house?" she asked.

"Close," Jack assured the nurse. "I'll go out first. When I motion for you to leave the house, move fast and get in the truck. Understand?"

The moment Lucille and Caroline nodded, Jack disengaged the security system and went out onto the porch. As he'd done at that kitchen window, he glanced around. So did Caroline, and she wished she had a gun or some other weapon that she could actually use with her still-weak hand. There was no chance of Jack giving her anything like that.

Because he didn't trust her.

She knew plenty about distrust and had spent every waking moment of the past year feeling the same thing. It'd been worse when she hadn't even known who she was. Well, in some ways it had been. Once she'd remembered, the distrust had collided with the fear that someone out there could still want her dead.

Not Jack.

She knew that now. But while she could trust him, she couldn't trust the others who were in his life. Part of her wanted to strike out on her own. But that would involve plenty of risks, too.

Still keeping watch, Jack went down the porch steps and started his truck. He motioned for them to move only after he threw open the passenger-side door.

"Now," he called out.

She and Lucille hurried off the porch, and even though it hadn't been Caroline's intention, she ended up in the middle of the seat, right next to Jack. Since she'd arrived at the safe house she had avoided touching him, but that was impossible now. They were shoulder to shoulder and hip to hip.

Jack immediately hit the accelerator, and while he continued glancing around them, he made a call using the control on his steering wheel. A few seconds later, a woman answered.

"Teagan," Jack said.

Caroline knew that was his partner, Marshal Teagan Randolph. She'd heard Jack give Lucille the marshal's contact info in case there was an emergency and she couldn't reach Jack. That meant he must trust the woman, but Caroline didn't want anyone else brought into this just yet. She was about to tell him that, too, but he cursed before Teagan or she could say anything.

"What's wrong?" Teagan immediately asked.

"We have a tail," Jack spat out. "I'm on the east farm road about twelve miles from Longview Ridge. I need backup right now."

Chapter Three

The moment Jack said someone was following them, Caroline jerked her body around to look out the back window of his truck. She groaned, no doubt seeing exactly what Jack had caught sight of.

A black four-door sedan with a heavily tinted windshield.

The fact that it was a car made it stand out in a place where most folks drove trucks. Maybe a crazed groupie/killer wannabe hadn't gotten the memo on that, and had failed to blend in.

Jack hadn't had a choice about requesting backup. He'd noticed the sedan pulling out of a ranch trail just moments after he had driven past it. Of course, it was possible this wasn't someone after Caroline, that it was just a driver in the wrong place at the wrong time, maybe even someone who'd gotten lost, but Jack couldn't risk not having an extra gun if something bad went down. Or rather, if something *worse* was going down.

The *bad* had already happened.

There was no scenario Jack could come up with that made Kingston Morris showing up just yards from the safe house a good thing. Which was why he should have called for backup even sooner. Unfortunately, Jack had let himself get distracted with Caroline's bombshell. Now that he'd remembered he was a lawman and not her former lover—or the son of a murdered sheriff—he would press her more on why she'd lied. Press her more, too, on the bits of so-called evidence from the night his dad had been killed. For now, Jack just kept an eye on the car behind them.

"Are Caroline and Lucille okay?" Teagan asked. "Are *you* okay?"

"So far." Jack wanted it to stay that way.

"Do you think it's that guy, Kingston Morris, who you asked me to run?" Teagan added.

"Possibly." But the more honest answer would be "Yes." It would be hard to believe it was a coincidence that an Eric groupie to appeared on a security camera and then someone else showed up on this remote stretch of the road.

"There's no immediate threat," Jack added to his partner, "but I want backup in place."

"Understood."

Jack opened his mouth to give Teagan some instructions as to what he needed her to do, but Caroline tugged on his arm to get his attention. At first he thought that was because she'd seen the person behind that dark windshield, but she merely stared at him. No one had ever accused him of having ESP or even being tuned in to nonverbal cues, but he got this one all right.

Caroline didn't want him to mention that she'd gotten her memory back. Since he couldn't see why Teagan would need to know that right at this exact moment, Jack nodded. Obviously Caroline was good with the nonverbal, too, because she blew out a breath of relief.

"I need you to run the plates on a black sedan for me," Jack continued with Teagan. He could hear his partner typing away on her keyboard. No doubt arranging for the backup he'd requested. But she could multitask, too, so he rattled off the license plate number to her.

"It's a rental car," Teagan said just moments later. "I'll find out who rented it."

Jack was betting the person who'd done that had used an alias. Well, unless Kingston or the person in the sedan was truly an idiot. That wouldn't make this situation less dangerous, because Jack knew from experience that idiots could kill just as well as smart people. The idiots just didn't tend to get away with it, but that didn't make their victims less dead or instances like this any less lethal.

The seconds seemed to drag before Teagan came back on the line. "Lee Zeller's in the field about twenty miles from you. He's the closest marshal for backup."

Jack kept his speed at a steady pace and considered his options. Zeller wasn't one of them, and he glanced at Caroline to see if she agreed. Judging from the way her forehead creased, she did. Which meant she'd been doing some investigating and had likely hacked her way through the filters in multiple files.

He was getting better at picking up the unspoken stuff.

"Bad choice for backup?" Teagan asked Jack when he didn't respond.

Teagan could read him. She'd been Jack's partner for two years and had read all the files on his father's murder.

Zeller had been involved in an investigation that Jack's father was running at the time he was gunned down. Sex trafficking. Zeller hadn't been a suspect in that case. Heck, there'd been no hints of any wrongdoing on his part, but Jack didn't like the way these particular lines had intersected. Because it would only rattle Caroline even more, he didn't want anyone from his father's investigations playing backup for him.

Well, no one who wasn't family.

That was going to tighten Caroline's forehead, too, and break some rules, but that car behind them certainly wasn't putting her at ease, either. Ditto for Lucille. Both women had turned to watch it again.

"I need to make another call," he told Teagan. "Get me the name on the rental car." Jack hung up and hit the button on his steering wheel.

"Call Kellan," he instructed his phone.

As expected, Caroline whirled back around while shaking her head. Frantically shaking it. There was no need for her to repeat her warning that while she thought she could trust Jack, she didn't feel that way about other cops. Or anyone else with a badge and a police radio who could maybe listen in on their conversation. So, while he waited for the call to his brother to connect, he gave her proof for why she should want Kellan in on this.

Jack sped up.

So did the car behind them.

When he slowed, the sedan followed suit. It let Caroline know that there could be a real threat behind them. Maybe it was Kingston. Maybe hired guns paid for with Kingston's trust fund. It could be someone who wasn't even on their radar, who'd used Kingston as a dupe.

Whatever this was, this situation could get

ugly. In fact, the only reason it probably hadn't already was because the driver was waiting until they reached the road leading to Longview Ridge. It was wider and didn't coil around like a rattlesnake. It would be easier to make a move there. Jack was guessing the guy might try to run them off the road or else shoot at them.

Caroline's eyes were already wide, and only grew bigger when she saw how closely the sedan was mirroring their moves. Lucille saw it, too, and she threw her small suitcase on the floor of the truck, no doubt to free up her hands. She drew her gun just as Kellan answered the phone.

"You're on speaker," Jack warned his brother right off. "And I have Caroline and Lucille in the truck with me."

"What happened?" Kellan snapped.

"Kingston Morris, a possible groupie connected to Eric, showed up at the safe house, and now I think he could be following us. And no, you won't find his name in our files. That's because Caroline only told me about him less than a half hour ago. Apparently, Kingston visited Caroline's office while Eric was there, and Kingston made a strong enough impression for her to remember him."

Jack paused to give his brother a second to let that sink in. It sank in quickly.

"She got her memory back," Kellan concluded, and without even taking a breath, he added, "Dad's killer?"

Jack had anticipated that would be the first of his brother's questions. "She claims she doesn't know."

Jack figured the skepticism in his wording was going to piss her off, and it did. But he didn't care. She'd lied to him. And while her lie might not be responsible for the car following them, if he'd known the facts—all of them—he might have been able to pick up Kingston before it even came to this.

Even without having the details spelled out for him, it obviously riled Kellan, too, because he cursed. "Where are you? You need backup?"

"Yes to the backup." Jack gave Kellan his location. "I'm heading to your office, so meet me."

Jack didn't wait for his brother's assurance that he would do just that. No need. Kellan would get there as fast as he could. Maybe it would be fast enough, but Jack didn't like the bad feeling that was slithering its way down his back. That turn with the straighter, wider road was coming up fast.

"You know how I feel involving your brothers in this," Caroline snapped the moment he was off the phone with Kellan. "They could trust fellow cops who are dirty."

"Lesser of two evils," Jack reminded her, and just to prove his point, he slowed down. The sedan kept pace.

She made a sound to indicate she was considering what he'd said, but she didn't argue. Caroline twisted back around to keep watch.

Jack considered just flooring the accelerator and trying to outrace this moron. But that was risky. Curvy roads could lead to accidents, which would in turn make them sitting ducks. Plus, the sedan engine might be souped-up enough that it wouldn't have any trouble catching up with them. Jack wanted to delay the showdown until Kellan was closer.

"Who's Marshal Zeller?" Lucille asked. Her voice was a little shaky. So was she. But she was holding her own and didn't look ready to panic. "Why didn't you want him for backup?"

"Because he could be dirty," Caroline grumbled before Jack could say anything.

As answers went, it was a pretty good one. In her mind, Zeller could indeed be dirty. The jury was still out on that for Jack, but if there'd been any red flags to find, Jack figured he would have found them by now. That was because he'd dug and dug deep. Not just on Zeller but on any-and everyone connected to his father's investigations.

"Zeller headed a sex-trafficking case that

popped a little over a year ago," Jack told Lucille. Like the women, he still had his eyes on the sedan. "One that involved some college students. One of those students, Nicola Gunderson, was abducted from a diner in Longview Ridge, and then she turned up dead. That's how my dad got involved. My brother Kellan too, since he was a deputy at the time."

"Oh, yes. I remember." Lucille's voice was a little tight, but Jack knew that wasn't because she had something to hide or even any personal knowledge of the case. However, she did have plenty of knowledge about sex offenses since she'd been a victim of a violent rape fifteen years earlier.

Zeller wasn't the only person Jack had vetted all the way down to ground zero.

Jack hadn't considered Lucille's past a concern, but rather he saw how she responded to it by cultivating her current assets. She'd learned to protect herself and continued her nursing career, and Jack figured that was a bonus skill set when it came to choosing who would be staying with Caroline. Right now, he appreciated that skill set very much, but he hoped he didn't need Lucille to play backup.

"You're taking me to the sheriff's office," Caroline concluded.

Jack couldn't figure out a way to sugarcoat it. "I am."

She sat there, obviously weighing her options as he'd done earlier. She was smart. Smart enough to keep her mouth shut about regaining her memory because she didn't know the snakes from the good guys. And that meant she'd soon figure out that the only choice she had was to go with him to the sheriff's office. That didn't mean she'd like it, though.

Jack had to slow down as he approached the last turn that would take him to town. They were about six miles out now.

Not far.

With Kellan no doubt already en route, it meant he had only a couple more minutes before he could do something about this tail. He wanted to question whoever was behind that wheel. If it was Kingston, he would question him even harder, because maybe he, too, had been at the abandoned hotel the night Jack's father was murdered.

Jack took the turn on the road, and while his attention hadn't strayed from the sedan, he watched it even closer now. Though he soon figured out there was no need for watching, because the driver immediately sped up.

Hell.

Kellan was still nowhere in sight, but Jack got

a glimpse of something he sure as heck didn't want to see. The driver's-side window of the sedan lowered. A hand came out. One holding a gun.

"Get down!" Jack shouted to Caroline and Lucille.

Not a second too soon. Because the shot slammed into the truck.

Chapter Four

Caroline ducked down and grabbed on to Lucille to make sure she did the same just as a bullet blasted through the truck's back window. The safety glass shattered, but the pieces that pummeled them had a plastic coating to keep them from being lethal or cutting them to shreds.

The second shot could fall into the lethal category, though.

It slammed into the driver's side of the glass, missing Jack's head by what appeared to be a fraction of an inch.

Fear roared through her, but so did anger. Whoever was doing his—Kingston, maybe—was putting Jack and Lucille in danger, all so he could get to her.

Of course, the flashbacks came. Nightmarish memories of the other attack, the gunfire the night Jack's father had been murdered. Jack was no doubt reliving some bad stuff, as well.

"I can hold the steering wheel so you can return fire," Caroline offered.

With narrowed eyes, he spared her a glance, looking at her as if she'd lost her mind. "You're staying down." And he caught onto her neck to push her lower. "I have no intention of confronting this jerk with Lucille and you in the vehicle. I'll do that later when it's just me and him."

Jack didn't leave any room for argument on that, and he hit the accelerator again just as the shooter sent a third bullet their way. Since Lucille was shaking and mumbling a prayer, Caroline put her arm around the woman to try to comfort her.

Mixed in with the sound of a fourth shot, Caroline heard something else. The howl of a police siren. It gave her a jolt of relief. Then, a wave of more fear. Because this was probably Kellan.

The shots stopped instantly, and behind them was the screech of brakes. When Jack cursed, she risked lifting her head to see what was going on. The shooter had stopped and was turning his car around.

No doubt so he could get away.

Jack pulled to the side of the road, and that was when Caroline looked out of the front of the truck and spotted not one but two cruisers. Two deputies were in one, and they sped past them, heading in pursuit of the gunman. Kellan was driving the second cruiser, and he pulled up next to Jack.

"Is anyone hurt?" Kellan immediately asked, glancing up at the shot-out glass, then his brother. Then, at Caroline. Kellan was probably good at poker, because she couldn't tell what he was thinking other than the obvious concern for his brother and them.

Jack made a quick check of her and Lucille, but his attention didn't stray far from his rearview mirror. Keeping watch for the sedan that had sped away from them.

"We're okay," Jack assured his brother. "I need to get them to the sheriff's office."

Kellan gave a quick nod. "I would have all of you get in the cruiser with me, but the guy might return, and I don't want you out in the open. I'll follow you back and send out another crew of deputies to assist in chasing down that car."

Jack matched his brother's nod and took off. "It'll only take us a couple of minutes to get there," Jack told Lucille and her.

Minutes. Not long before she could be walking into a lion's den. But then, as Jack had said, for her it was the lesser of two evils. She definitely didn't want to hang around, waiting for a gunman.

Those couple of minutes crawled by, and it

didn't help that Caroline had broken glass all over her. A reminder of the attack. God, when was this going to end? For over a year she had been fighting for her life, and now she'd apparently brought that fight straight to Jack.

Jack didn't slow down until his truck screeched to a stop in front of the sheriff's office. Kellan must have already called ahead, because another of Jack's brothers, Deputy Owen Slater, was in the open doorway, and he had his gun drawn. As soon as Kellan arrived he took Owen's place, and Owen drove off in the cruiser. No doubt in pursuit of the shooter.

"I called a medic," Kellan said as they all hurried inside. "He'll be here soon." Another of the deputies, Gunnar Pullam, immediately took hold of Lucille's arm. Caroline knew him, and had never gotten any criminal vibes from him, but she still kept her distance.

"Move away from the windows," Jack snapped.

Caroline didn't need a reminder of the danger or another slam of adrenaline, but Jack's words gave her both anyway.

Jack turned to Gunnar. "Do you want to take Lucille to the break room to wait for the medic?" he suggested.

"And after she gets checked out, take her statement," Kellan added.

When Kellan looked at Caroline this time, his face wasn't so poker ready. His mouth was tight, maybe because she hadn't remembered his father's killer. Or perhaps he just thought she hadn't wanted to tell him.

Caroline was certain there was some tightness in her mouth, too. Was she looking into the eyes of a killer? Maybe not. But it was possible that Kellan was covering for one.

With his hand still on her arm, Jack led her across the squad room that was jammed with desks and equipment and took her inside Kellan's office.

"Stay here," he told her and immediately went back out into the squad room, where Kellan waited.

The brothers were only about ten feet away from her, but Jack didn't exactly broadcast what he was saying, keeping his voice barely louder than a whisper. Still, Caroline caught a word here and there. *Three days ago, she said. Dirty cop. You. Yeah, she thinks that.*

The last one caused Kellan to huff and then scowl, but when he glanced over Jack's shoulder at her, the scowl disappeared. The look he gave her riled her to the core. Because it was pity. Kellan thought she was too damaged to think straight. He was dismissing her concerns that a lawman had been the one to help Eric in the attack a year ago.

Jack also glanced back at her, frowned and then mumbled something else to Kellan. She didn't catch a single word of that, but Jack started toward her. Not hurrying, but with every step he took, he kept his eyes on her.

When he reached her, she was about to blast him for spilling all to Kellan, but Jack stopped her with a touch. He pushed her hair from her face, examining her. Or so she thought until he extracted a blob of the safety glass, then another, from the top of her head.

Dragging in a weary breath, he closed the door, and in the same motion, he turned her to check the back of her hair. "Shake your clothes," he instructed. "Even safety glass can cut if you sit or lean back on it."

Her mouth got tighter, but she shook the dress and glass bits pinged to the tile floor. "You told your brother that I don't trust him," she snapped, "that I think he's a dirty cop involved in his father's murder."

Jack continued to pick off glass bits. "He would have figured it out. He's a lot better at body language than I am."

"You're fine with body language," she grumbled, but Caroline wished she'd kept that to herself.

She whirled around just in time to see him

smile that damnable smile, and she wasn't sure if she wanted to throttle him or kiss him. Caroline didn't do either, but it did cause her to freeze.

His next breath wasn't so much one of weariness as it was of relief. The long, lingering look he gave her made her think he was about to touch her again. He didn't. Instead, Jack crammed his hands into the pockets of his jeans.

"If you need to fall apart or cry, go ahead and do it," he offered. "You're shaking," he pointed out before she could insist she didn't intend to do either. She didn't know what she was stewing over more— Jack telling his brother her deep, dark fears or Kellan brushing it off as Jack had done to the glass.

But she was indeed trembling.

Her hands, her mouth. Heck, her legs. She was probably a breath away from both falling apart and crying.

"I nearly got Lucille and you killed," she said, and Caroline cursed her own voice. It was shaking, too.

Jack lifted an eyebrow. "Funny, I thought it was the shooter who nearly killed us."

"The shooter wouldn't have been firing those bullets if it hadn't been for me." She expected him to give her some sugarcoated answer, but she'd obviously forgotten this was Jack.

"That's true." With that hanging in the air, he waited a heartbeat. "And since I'd rather not have any more attempted murders, that means you're going to have to let me help you."

"You mean I'm going to have to trust Kellan," Caroline blurted out. She was feeling a lot less shaky now.

Jack shrugged, took his hand from his pocket so he could tap the badge on his belt. "Every lawman in Texas isn't tainted, and if you dig beneath all the anger, fear and whatever else it is you're feeling, you'll remember that I'm the best shot you've got at keeping us both alive."

He followed that too logical minilecture with a long stare. Jack was obviously waiting for her to come to the only conclusion that she had right now.

"I'm *not* going to trust your brother," she insisted, but left the rest of it unspoken—that she would trust Jack. Again, it was the only choice she had.

He nodded as if they'd just hashed that out with a heated argument. "I'll do whatever it takes to keep you safe." He paused. "Want me to take a bullet for you to prove it?"

Jack didn't wink, but he might as well have, because he was obviously trying to lighten things up. Trying to bring her back down and ease some of the still raw adrenaline. It was working, sort of, since it was something he'd said to her in jest when they'd been lovers. A way of letting her know that he cared that much for her.

"No," she said, drawing out the one-word answer to emphasize it. There was a lot more emotion in her voice than she wanted as she stared at him.

Thinking.

Remembering.

Yes, definitely remembering.

That helped more than his lame attempt at cop humor. His being there helped, too, and despite everything she'd been through—or maybe because of it—Caroline wanted to step right into his arms. Those strong arms with their toned muscles. She wanted to feel the heat, and the comfort that she'd gotten there before. Jack had tugged and pulled at her in a way that no man ever had before.

Or ever would again, she was forced to admit to herself.

Yes, it'd been great sex. The fire between them so hot. The feel of him touching her with those calloused hands. Him, being inside her. She'd felt that, too.

If it'd been just those things, *only those*, she could have pushed it all away. Could have distracted herself with the dark fear that was eating holes in her. But it had been more—way more—and she had to admit that to herself, too.

With those stormy gray eyes locked on hers, he reached up and touched his finger to the center of her forehead. Just a touch, maybe to her scar, the one that Eric had given her when he hit her. Or maybe Jack was trying to ease the tensed muscles there. And despite everything she'd just admitted to herself, Caroline still hadn't been prepared for that touch. For the way his warm breath fell on her. For the look of him.

That face. His eyes. His mouth that had fueled enough fantasies to last her a couple of lifetimes.

"Penny for your thoughts," he drawled. "A dollar for them if you're thinking about sex." The corner of his mouth hitched. Because he knew her thoughts, knew everything she was feeling right now.

Since he was feeling the same thing, Caroline laid her hand on his chest. Over his heart, which she could feel beating to the rhythm of hers.

"Sex won't help," she said, her voice mostly breath.

His slight smile stayed in place. A smile that only he and Mona Lisa could have pulled off. "That depends on the sex."

Jack made her laugh before she could stop

herself or remember there was absolutely nothing to laugh about. He hooked his arm around the back of her neck in a casual, easy way, and lowering his head to her, took her laugh with his mouth.

Kissing her.

It was like hot silk sliding through her. Oh, it felt wonderful. That incredible taste. Those clever moves, with seemingly no effort. He made no demands, and yet, also seemed to make the biggest demand of all. Within seconds, he had turned the hot silk to blazing flames.

"It's good to have you back," he whispered against her mouth.

Is it? she wanted to say. She'd brought nothing but trouble with her. But there wasn't time for her question because the door opened, and Kellan stepped in.

Jack moved away from her, but he took his time, which meant Kellan had no trouble seeing Jack's arm around her and their mouths hovering over each other. It didn't make Kellan a happy camper. He scowled at his brother.

"The medic's here to check Caroline," Kellan said, his attention nailed to Jack. "And I just spoke to Kingston on the phone, and he said he'd come in for questioning, to *set some things straight*. He's on his way here right now."

Chapter Five

Jack wanted to curse. Even though he probably should, he didn't regret kissing Caroline. But now he was going to have to listen to Kellan tell him why a kissing regret should be at the top of his list.

And Kellan would be right.

Caroline didn't look so much regretful as she did embarrassed. Nervous, too. That was likely because of the distrust she had for not only Kellan but all the other cops in the building.

"I'll find the medic," she muttered, moving past both Jack and Kellan to hurry away.

Kellan immediately motioned toward Sherry McNeil, one of the deputies at a desk in the squad room. "Keep an eye on her," Kellan said to Sherry, tipping his head in the direction of both Caroline and the ladies' room.

Jack just lifted an eyebrow.

"Caroline lied to you. She waited three days to tell you she'd gotten her memory back," Kellan said, as if that excused the tail he'd just put on her.

"She lied because she doesn't trust me. Not yet."

Kellan made a sound of disagreement. "She looked pretty trusting to me when she was kissing you."

"That was the attraction. It's always been intense between us."

He wouldn't tell his brother that Caroline and he had gone all night their first time together. As if they'd been starved for each other. Hell, they were still starved for each other. If the door had been locked and Kellan hadn't walked in, Jack might have backed Caroline against the wall and taken her then and there.

And she would have let him.

He'd felt that. The way her body had hummed against his. His own body had hummed plenty, too, and Jack knew it wasn't going to be easy to rein in that kind of heat. And he doubted he would be able to count on an interruption to give him the willpower to resist a woman he'd never been able to resist.

"I don't have to tell you this, but I will," Kellan went on a moment later. "Sex could cause you to lose focus."

This was obviously going to be one of the big topics of conversation today. "Lack of sex can do that, too. I haven't been with another woman since Caroline." Jack looked at Kellan then but didn't see even one raised eyebrow. "You don't seem surprised."

"I'm not just a cop, I'm also your big brother. I know you fell hard for her, but she's not the same woman she was a year ago."

"Of course, she's not," Jack snapped. "She was nearly murdered by a serial killer and had amnesia. Hard to come back from that. But Caroline's there. Underneath the tangled mess of memories in her head, she's there."

The sound that Kellan made was still edged with suspicion. "Personally, I like her. There's plenty of toughness beneath that delicate-looking exterior."

Yes, there was, and it was one of the things that had first attracted Jack to her. But her toughness had some fractures in it now. Thanks to Eric. This latest attack sure wasn't going to help, either.

Jack scrubbed his hand over his face. "I need to figure out how the location of the WITSEC house was breached, and I have to look into those things that Caroline heard the night Dad was killed."

Kellan's jaw tightened. "The police radio transmissions. The mention of this office. The dispatch codes." He glanced around the squad room. "I'll help with that. I trust every person who works for me, but I won't blow off what Caroline told you. That's why I sent Sherry to keep an eye on her. Caroline said the voice on that call to Eric was male, so she should be okay with Sherry watching after her."

Jack sent his brother a silent look of thanks for that.

"The call Caroline heard could have been part of the sick game that Eric was playing," Kellan added after a pause. "Something to throw her off the accomplice who was actually helping him."

That wasn't just possible. It was likely. The trouble would be to convince Caroline of that, and his best shot at doing it was to figure out how Eric could have faked a call like that.

When Jack heard someone clear their throat, he looked to the doorway and saw Tatum Carson, the medic. "Neither of the women has any injuries," Tatum told them, "but if you want me to take them into the hospital for tests, I will."

"No," Lucille and Caroline said in unison. They were behind the medic, and Sherry and Gunnar stood behind them.

Jack looked at both Lucille and Caroline and knew there'd be no other tests. "Thanks. You can go," he said to Tatum.

With a suit-yourself shrug, the medic gathered his things and headed out.

"Lucille wants to go to her sister's in San Antonio," Gunnar said, stepping up. "I got her statement and her contact info. Her sister doesn't have a car, so Lucille will need a ride. Is it okay for her to go?"

This was touchy jurisdictional territory. The shooting hadn't happened at the WITSEC safe house, which meant technically this was Kellan's case. Jack didn't want to cross any gray lines—when he managed to make an arrest, he needed to have dotted all the i's and crossed all the t's to get a conviction. He also didn't want to step on his brother's toes, so he looked at Kellan, wanting him to respond to Gunnar's question.

"Any chance this shooter will go after Lucille?" Kellan asked Jack.

"Slim to none." Caroline was the target. Jack was certain of that. "But San Antonio PD should be alerted just in case something comes up. That way, they can make sure Lucille is protected."

"She can leave," Kellan said, apparently satisfied with what Jack had just told him. "I can't send Gunnar with her, though, because he's got to testify in court in about an hour. He won't make it back here in time. Sherry, will you drive Lucille and contact SAPD on the way there?"

Sherry nodded, and, as the medic had done, the deputy started to gather her things, too. However, Lucille didn't budge. Instead, she caught onto Caroline's shoulders and looked her straight in the eyes.

"Remember what I taught you," Lucille said.

Caroline nodded. "Open-hand strike to the nose, followed by a hard kick to the groin."

Jack winced, but Lucille smiled, clearly proud of her student. She brushed a kiss on Caroline's cheek, whispered a goodbye and headed out with the deputy.

"Should I take Caroline's statement now?" Gunnar asked.

This was another t-crossing and i-dotting moment. Since Jack had also been on the receiving end of that attack, he couldn't question her. Heck, he shouldn't even be in the room with her during the interview. That meant Caroline was about to be questioned by a male cop whom she maybe didn't trust.

Jack was still mulling over the best way to handle that when he realized the interview and his own mulling were going to have to wait. That was because he saw a now familiar face had stepped into the squad room.

Kingston walked in, and he was wearing the same clothes he'd had on in the security footage. What the footage hadn't captured was the cocky look on his face. It appeared to be a permanent expression.

"Caroline," Kingston purred, his attention going straight to her. "So you're still alive. Too bad that you won't be that way for long."

CAROLINE PULLED BACK her shoulders. Considering Kingston had been friends with a serial killer, she hadn't expected him to look, well, normal, but she also hadn't believed he'd come waltzing into a sheriff's office to dole out what sounded like a threat.

"I'm Kingston Morris," he greeted as if this were a social call. He thrust out his hand for Jack to shake. "And you're Marshal Slater. Good to meet you."

Jack didn't exchange handshakes, but he gave Kingston a look that could have frozen Hades. He caught onto Kingston, whirled him around and, despite the man's howl of protest, frisked him. No weapon.

"*So you're still alive. Too bad that you won't be that way for long,*" Jack growled, repeating word for word what Kingston had just said. "Along with some other things, you'll want to explain that *now*."

Kingston was wise enough to drop the cocky smile and the protest over the pat down, but he didn't appear as concerned as he should be, considering that Jack looked ready to tear him limb from limb.

"I said that because of the attack." There wasn't much concern in Kingston's voice, either. *Unflappable* was the word that came to Caroline's mind. "Lots of gossip about it, and from what people are saying, someone wanted to kill Caroline and you."

Now Kingston turned to her, their gazes connecting, and Caroline forced herself not to take a step back. Too bad that he spurred the old memories, and she got a burst of the flashbacks before she could stop them. The pain and the fear. She'd thought she was going to die, and the swarm of emotions that had come with that belief hit her now.

Jack must have noticed or else guessed about the flashbacks, because he moved closer to her, his arm brushing against her. It was surprising and unnerving how just a simple touch from him could soothe her. But Caroline would take it. She definitely didn't want to collapse into a puddle from a panic attack when she needed to confront Kingston.

"You tried to kill Jack and me?" Caroline came out and asked, and she made sure she held eye contact with Kingston.

"No, of course not." It sounded more mocking than genuine, but at least the man started to show some concern when Jack turned on a recorder and began to read him his rights.

"You're arresting me?" Kingston demanded several times while he was Mirandized.

"Any reason I shouldn't?" Jack countered after he'd finished. "You were at Caroline's not long before she was attacked."

Jack didn't add more to that explanation, and Caroline thought she knew why. He was giving Kingston a chance to lie by denying it. If so, that would add weight to his arrest.

However, Kingston shrugged. "Yes, I was there," he readily admitted. "I got a text, giving me the address and saying I should go there."

Jack eased up on the glare to give the man a look of skepticism. Caroline felt the same way, and when Kingston obviously picked up on their disbelief, he huffed and took out his phone. After he'd pulled up a message, he handed Jack his phone.

There it was on the screen. No name of the person who'd sent the message, but there was the address of the safe house, along with the message, Want to get a look at the woman who helped kill your friend Eric Lang? You'll find her here.

"I don't know who sent it, and the number is no longer working," Kingston explained. "My guess is he or she used a disposable cell and deactivated it."

"Or else you used such a phone and sent the message to yourself," Jack quickly countered.

Kingston didn't exactly give him an eye roll, but it was close. "There's no reason for me to do that."

Jack didn't waste any time arguing. "Sure there is. You might think a message like that would get you off the hook. It won't. You were in the vicinity of Caroline's house, and you have a motive to murder her."

"A motive?" Kingston challenged. "You mean because of Eric?" He didn't wait for Jack to confirm or deny that. "I wouldn't kill because of him. Yes, I was intrigued by Eric. He was very interesting and charismatic, but I wouldn't have done his bidding. Besides, he's dead."

Jack leveled his gaze on Kingston. "Yet you acted on what you're saying was an anonymous tip to go to the house of a woman you blame for the death of this interesting and charismatic piece of dirt?"

Kingston opened his mouth, then closed it as if rethinking what he'd been about to say. "I don't blame Caroline for Eric's death." He shifted his attention to Kellan. "I believe you're the one who delivered what eventually became the fatal blow."

"I did," Kellan readily admitted. "I just wish I'd been able to put a bullet in him sooner."

If Kingston had a reaction to that, he didn't show it. Instead, he turned back to Caroline. "Someone wants you dead. The attack proves that. And I think the person who sent me that message thought I'd do the job for him or her."

"Do you want to do the job?" Caroline asked, and thankfully she sounded a lot tougher than she felt. More of those flashbacks bolted through her like lightning, and for just a moment she wished she hadn't recovered those parts of her memory.

Again, Kingston took his time answering. "There's no law against admiring a man like Eric. In his own twisted way, he was a genius. And he kept you alive. That's a key point here. Why would I want to go against him on that? If he didn't kill you, then why should I?"

Caroline didn't have to think long to come up with a reason. A sick one. "Because he's dead, and you might want the thrill of murdering me to honor a man who intrigued you."

"No." Kingston looked her straight in the eyes when he said that. "I wouldn't do that, and I'm not responsible for the attack against you. I merely went to your place out of curiosity."

Caroline wasn't sure she believed that, but the problem would be finding the proof.

Maybe they'd get that with the rental car. Jack had asked his brother, Texas Ranger Eli Slater, to assist with locating it, though she was concerned that Kingston had covered his tracks there. Strange, though, that he hadn't done the same track-covering at the safe house. But then maybe he hadn't known there'd be security cameras at the back of the property.

"Did you send Eric money the night he took Caroline hostage?" Jack asked Kingston. Obviously, he intended to press the man on more than just the attack. Of course, anything Jack found out about Kingston could give them more fodder to make an arrest.

"I did," Kingston admitted, "but I didn't know what he'd done. It hadn't hit the news yet that Caroline had been taken hostage, and Eric didn't mention it."

Eric hadn't. Caroline had been there for that entire call, and not once had Eric said anything about why he needed funds.

"How'd you get him the money?" Jack pressed.

"I gathered the cash. Ten grand. It was all my parents had in their safe. I put it in a bag and left it for Eric on the side of the road where he told me to leave it."

Jack gave Kingston another dose of his lawman's glare. "And you didn't think it was a little strange that a person you knew or at least suspected was a serial killer would ask you for money?"

"No. I didn't know or suspect he was a serial killer," Kingston insisted. "That didn't come out until later, until he escaped with Caroline."

Maybe. But Caroline still wasn't buying it.

"Did you get Eric a car that night, too?" Jack continued.

Caroline had to speak up on this. "No. Eric stole it. Or rather, he had me hot-wire it. It was in the driveway of a house not far from the abandoned inn where your father was killed." She paused, stared at Kingston. "But just because you didn't do that doesn't make you an innocent man."

"No, it doesn't," Kellan agreed before Kingston could respond. "I need to take him to the interview room and get his statement." He didn't invite Jack and her to go with him. No doubt because it would be a conflict of interest since Kingston was a suspect in their attack. Still, Caroline wanted to hear what else the man had to say.

"There's an observation room," Jack told her, and they headed out of the office and toward the hall.

However, they hadn't made it far before the front door opened again. This time, it wasn't a suspect who came in but Gemma. In the blink of an eye, the past months melted away, and Caroline felt the warmth of seeing a dear friend. Even though she figured the flashbacks would soon return, she savored the moment when Gemma rushed to her and pulled her into her arms.

"You're okay?" Gemma muttered.

Caroline nodded. It wasn't the total truth, but she hadn't been physically harmed. That was what Gemma needed to know for now.

When Gemma pulled back, Caroline saw tears in her friend's eyes. Not just from the relief of her not being injured but because her memory had returned. Gemma didn't have to say that aloud for Caroline to know that Kellan had told her.

Jack cleared his throat to get their attention. "I'm going to the observation room. Why don't you two talk in Jack's office?"

Only then did Caroline remember that they were too close to the windows. Not a good idea for either one of them. Caroline hooked her arm around Gemma's waist and got her moving.

"How much have you remembered?" Gemma asked.

"Enough." Caroline didn't say more until they were in the office. "I got my memory back three days ago."

Gemma nodded. Then she sighed. Obviously, her friend didn't understand why Caroline had kept it a secret. Heck, Gemma might not even understand after she'd explained. Still, Caroline had to try.

"Eric made a call to someone the night he took me hostage. I heard a police radio in the background. I heard someone say Longview Ridge. The caller used cop words, including dispatch codes. I know, I know," Caroline added before Gemma could try to explain all of that away. "It doesn't mean Kellan's guilty. But he could be unknowingly shielding a killer because he can't see past his friendships or blind loyalty to the badge."

Much to Caroline's surprise, Gemma didn't dismiss that. "So you think it could be one of Kellan's deputies? Or Jack?"

"Not Jack." Caroline should have at least hesitated a split second. "He might have that badge blindness—" or DNA blindness, she silently added, when it came to his brothers "—but Jack doesn't want me dead."

Gemma was one of the best profilers that she'd ever met, and she turned those profiling eyes on Caroline. And she waited as if she knew Caroline was holding something back.

She was.

Of course, Gemma knew about her history

with Jack. Knew all about Jack and her being lovers.

"I kissed Jack," Caroline blurted out, cursing herself. She added some more curse words for Jack, too.

"And you think that was a...wise idea?" Gemma asked as if carefully choosing her words.

"No! Of course, it wasn't. It was the worst idea in the history of bad ideas. Someone's trying to kill me. I don't know who to trust, and I feel ready to unravel. The whole time I'm feeling all of that, I'm thinking how can a man like Jack still want me when I'm like this?" Caroline paused, steadied herself and admitted the truth. "But he did want me. As much as I wanted him."

Gemma sighed and took hold of her shoulders. "You can trust him. And you can trust Kellan, though I don't expect you to just take my word for it."

"I'm sorry I can't take your word for it." Caroline scrubbed her hand over her face. "I really am ready to unravel."

"Yes, I can see that. Just be careful not to unravel in Jack's arms."

That sent Caroline's gaze back to Gemma. "You can't believe Jack would want to hurt me."

"No, I don't, but I think he could hurt you

here." She tapped her fingers on Caroline's heart. "Hurt himself, too. Caring this much doesn't always help. Just take things as slow as you can. Keep your mind open." Gemma blinked back more tears, then smiled. "And for Pete's sake, quit aiming your suspicious eyes at the man I love."

Gemma's smile didn't last, though, and Caroline could see the concern return to her friend's expression. Caroline figured she was about to get a lecture about staying safe and cooperating with Kellan and Jack, but Gemma stopped when Jack appeared in the office doorway.

"We have a visitor," Jack said, and judging from his tone, it wasn't someone he especially wanted to see.

Caroline moved closer to him so she could peer over his shoulder, and she saw the tall, lean man making his way toward them. Correction—not just a man, but a marshal.

Marshal Lee Zeller.

The very person that Jack hadn't trusted enough to give them backup when the sedan was following them.

"There was no need for you to come," Jack quickly told Zeller.

But Zeller shook his head. "I need to talk to you," he said. "Because I think I might know who's trying to kill Caroline."

Chapter Six

Until Zeller had said that last sentence, Jack had been about to demand that the marshal get the heck out of there. But that stopped him.

Because I think I might know who's trying to kill Caroline.

Jack put on hold his demand for Zeller to leave and gave the man his full attention. He definitely wanted to hear what Zeller had to say, but he'd take every one of the marshal's words with a grain of salt. That was because underneath it all, Jack didn't trust him.

"I'm listening," Caroline prompted when Zeller didn't add anything else. She sounded steady enough. Maybe even a little riled. But Jack knew her nerves were right there at the surface.

Zeller dragged in a heavy breath, put his hands on his hips and stared at Caroline. "I heard about the breach of security at the WIT-SEC house and about the attack. Are you okay?"

"Obviously not," Jack answered for her. "Someone's trying to kill her, and you just said you might know who that is. Spill it."

When Zeller shifted his attention back to Jack, the man's eyes were slightly narrowed. Probably because he didn't like Jack's prickly attitude. Tough. Jack wasn't going to ease up until he had some answers.

"Well, it's not me who wants her harmed, if that's what you're thinking," Zeller spat out. "I'm here to help, and maybe then you'll start to trust me again. I wear the same badge you do, remember?"

Zeller had likely said that to try to reassure Caroline that she was in safe hands, but considering what she'd overheard with Eric's phone call, Jack figured it had the opposite effect.

"Lily Terrell," Zeller tossed out there, and he let the name hang in the air.

Jack knew who she was, of course. He knew plenty of the names of people connected to his father's investigation, and Lily was one of them. For that matter, so was Zeller. Zeller and his father had been bumping heads over the sex-trafficking case they had both been looking into around the same time his dad was murdered. Jack still had some niggling doubts that those confrontations with Zeller or the investigation itself had led to his father's death, but what was missing was evidence of that.

"You think Lily Terrell is trying to kill me?" Caroline asked, her tone proving that she could sound just as grouchy as Jack.

Zeller sure didn't jump to say yes. "I think someone in her organization could be responsible," he answered, and Jack didn't think it was his imagination that the man had chosen his words carefully.

It'd been a while since Jack had read anything about Lily, but he could still recall plenty of the details. Lily Terrell was a millionaire heiress from San Antonio. Her organization, New Beginnings, ran a counseling center and residential facility for the girls and women rescued from the sex-trafficking ring that Zeller and Jack's father were investigating.

Jack glanced at Caroline. It was clear from her earlier question that she knew who Lily was. Of course, with her hacking skills, she had likely filled in whatever memory gaps she had.

Jack turned back to Zeller. "You have proof that Lily or someone she knows could be linked to what happened to Caroline?"

"No proof," Zeller readily admitted, "but there's something off at New Beginnings. I've been keeping tabs on it."

Jack could see why Zeller would do that. The

killer of Nicola Gunderson, one of the girls who'd been trafficked, had never been identified. With all the leads gone cold, Zeller might believe someone at the facility knew something about it.

"A woman has gone missing from New Beginnings," Zeller went on. "I know that doesn't mean she's dead. She could have just left." He shook his head, grumbling some profanity under his breath. "But what if Lily started that place because she was the one behind the sex-trafficking ring? She could have done that to make sure she could squash any incriminating info that could have come out about her."

Jack wasn't surprised, but he saw Caroline's eyes widen. He'd actually played around with that idea. Call him a first-class cynic, but it made him suspicious when someone like Lily made a grand gesture out of the goodness of their heart. Within hours of the sex-trafficking ring being busted, Lily had come forward with her offer to help the girls.

"Tell me about the missing woman," Jack said to Zeller.

Zeller didn't hesitate. "Her name is Skylar Greer. She'd been a runaway when she was lured into sex trafficking. Skylar was eighteen when she was rescued. She went to New Beginnings because she had no other place to go, and she went missing last month."

"Lily reported it?" Jack asked.

Now there was a pause. "No, she said Skylar just left. Like I said, I've been keeping tabs on the place, and I have someone inside I've been paying for info. A handyman named Bennie Darnell. Bennie claims he heard no talk of the girl wanting to go, but he did overhear Skylar talking about finding out who'd murdered Nicola Gunderson."

Now, that was interesting how it'd circled back to his father and his investigation. Well, it was interesting if it was true.

"Skylar had apparently gotten to know Nicola in the short time she was in the sex-trafficking ring," Zeller went on, "and Skylar wanted justice for her." He shifted his attention to Caroline. "Lily ticks some boxes on the profiling scale when it comes to something like this."

Zeller had obviously assumed that Caroline's memory was clear when it came to her profiling skill set. It was, but Jack didn't like that Zeller had seemed to know that. It made him wonder if Zeller had kept tabs on Caroline, as well.

"What boxes?" Caroline asked.

"For one thing, Lily has a record. Her folks paid plenty of money to make the trouble go away, but she had a fondness for drugs when she was a teenager. She wasted away a good chunk of her trust fund and then fell in with some girls who bilked money out of rich old men."

Caroline lifted her shoulder. "A criminal past doesn't necessarily mean you'll grow up to run your own sex-trafficking ring."

"No, but I have it on good word that Lily's stayed in touch with her criminal friends."

Still, that was a stretch, and Caroline's huff let Jack know they felt the same way about the information Zeller was giving them. It could be pertinent. *Could be.* Or it could be a smoke screen.

"Lily hasn't been arrested since she was a teenager," Jack reminded Zeller. "Everything indicates that she's not only turned her life around but that she also wants to help others."

But Jack was just playing devil's advocate on that, since Lily's life turnaround could indeed be a facade. From what he'd read, Lily was getting lots of charitable donations from her rich friends for New Beginnings, although she'd pumped in some money of her own. That meant a place like that could merely be a sweet tax shelter for her and nothing more.

"Bennie thinks there's something shady going on there," Zeller continued, "and for now I agree with him. I'll keep digging into Skylar's disappearance. Will do the same for Lily, too, and I'll let you know what I find out."

Jack nodded. He wasn't going to refuse information, but he would darn sure consider the source. A source who could want to get attention off himself and place it onto someone else like Lily.

Zeller snorted, his gaze sliding back and forth between them. "And you're not buying anything I'm saying. You have a different angle on who could be responsible for the attack today?" That question snapped out like a bullwhip.

Jack debated how much he would say, but he knew it wouldn't be long before Zeller heard about the man Kellan had in the interview room. Besides, if Jack was the one to tell Zeller, then he could watch his reaction.

"Kingston Morris showed up at Caroline's WITSEC house shortly before the attack," Jack explained.

Zeller shrugged. If he recognized Kingston's name, he didn't show any signs of it. Of course, he could be faking his reaction, but Jack hoped that it meant Zeller hadn't extended his "keeping tabs" to background checks like the ones Jack and Teagan had made. If Zeller was clean, Jack didn't mind the marshal knowing what they were up to, but the jury was still out on whether or not Zeller was dirty.

"Kingston was one of Eric's admirers," Jack went on a moment later.

Now Zeller's eyes widened and he cursed. "How the hell did he get the address?"

"To be determined. Kellan is questioning him now."

Zeller belted out more profanity. "The marshals should be doing that. A breach of security at a WITSEC house is our jurisdiction."

"Yeah, but the attack happened on Kellan's turf," Jack quickly reminded him. "Three counts of attempted murder trumps a trespassing charge. Plus, Kingston didn't try to break into the house. He just showed up on the security feed and then left."

Of course, Kingston had perhaps left so he'd be in position to fire those shots at Caroline, Lucille and him, but that was only speculation. Maybe Kellan was getting something from Kingston that would qualify as proof so they could arrest the man.

Zeller checked his watch. "I have to leave and help with a prisoner transport," he grumbled. "But I want to know if Kingston gives you anything."

Jack just lifted an eyebrow and waited for Zeller to tell him why he had a need for that kind of information.

"Caroline's attack could be linked to Nicola

Gunderson's murder." Zeller ground out the words, clearly not pleased that he was having to explain himself. "Nicola's killer was never caught, and I want to clear the case along with finding Skylar."

Jack wasn't ruling out that all of those events could be connected, but some of the pieces didn't have obvious fits. Kingston, for one. There was nothing to prove he was involved in the sex trafficking. For that matter, Caroline wasn't connected to it, either. Unless, of course, all of this went back to Eric. Maybe Eric had been working with the sex trafficker, and now the person or people behind that wanted to tie up loose ends. If someone thought Caroline was a loose end, that would be motive for the attack.

Zeller checked his watch again and moved as if to leave, but then he stopped and looked at Caroline. "Did you really get your memory back?"

Jack couldn't tell if that was a good guess or if Zeller had heard that from Teagan.

"Some of it," Caroline said.

As answers went, it was a darn good one. Evasive but also probing, because Jack was pretty sure Caroline was studying Zeller to gauge his reaction. However, Zeller didn't give them a chance to study much of anything. He turned away, heading for the door.

"Good," Zeller told her from over his shoulder. "I'll keep you both posted if I find out anything more about Lily."

Caroline and Jack stood there and watched as he left. "What do you think Zeller really wanted?" she asked.

Despite his bone-weary fatigue and frustration, Jack nearly smiled. He'd forgotten just how sharp Caroline could be and how she tended to think like a cop.

Or a criminal.

"I'm not sure," Jack said, "but it felt like a fishing expedition with some mud throwing for good measure. Don't worry. I don't trust him."

The slight sound she made seemed to be approval, but when she dodged his gaze, Jack stepped in front of her, forcing eye contact. Not very smart, considering the last time he'd done that they'd ended up kissing, but he wanted to see what was going on in the depths of her cool green eyes.

Plenty was going on.

Like him, she was tired and a little unsteady. Riled, too. She'd been through so much already and didn't deserve another attempt to murder her. Worse, Jack couldn't guarantee her that there wouldn't be another attack. Which was why he had to take precautions: losing her again wasn't an option.

He hadn't meant for his gaze to stay locked with hers. Also hadn't meant for the regret about the attack and then the heat to creep into his expression. Of course, with Caroline there was always heat, so it was hard not to have it playing into things. Impossible for her not to pick up on it, either.

"I can't kiss you again," she insisted. Then she huffed. "Well, I could, but I'm asking you to back off. I need room to breathe. Time to think."

Jack immediately stepped back, giving her that space and nearly smiling again when it seemed as if she was disappointed that another kiss hadn't happened. But she was right. They definitely needed some thinking time on this. Better yet, this called for some concentration coupled with plenty of detective work.

He scrubbed his hand over his face, dragged in a breath and started laying out some things. "Kellan should have enough probable cause on Kingston to get a look at his financials. That's a start. Also, I can arrange to have Kingston's friends interviewed just to see how deep his obsession with Eric went."

Caroline nodded. "I can help. Not by hacking into Kingston's bank records," she quickly added when he scowled at her. "But I can call the various research assistants that Gemma and I worked with and see if they remember anyone other than Kingston coming in with Eric. It's possible Kingston had some help if he put this attack together."

True, and searching for that might help Caroline keep her mind off the flashbacks and the panic attacks.

"What about Zeller?" she asked. "Is there any chance you can get into his financials?"

"Slim to none, with what I have on him. Which is nothing." Jack paused. "But he's not the only one who can talk to Lily and others at New Beginnings. Maybe Lily can shed some light on why Zeller has her in his sights for a whole boatload of felonies, including coming after you."

"I'd like to hear what she has to say. And no, I don't recall Eric mentioning anything about the sex trafficking, but he did have contact with a lot of bad people. Stupid, gullible people that he could charm into doing what he wanted," she added. "Look at what Kingston was willing to do for him. Maybe there are others who overlap with Lily, Eric and Kingston."

It was one of those angles that had to be checked out, but it would also be a big time suck. Jack was worried that time wasn't on Caroline's and his side right now. The person who'd attacked her would almost certainly come after her again.

He was about to suggest they go to the observation room to watch the rest of Kingston's interview, but Jack spotted his brother Eli coming in through the front door. Jack also saw Caroline stiffen, and he didn't have to guess why. She didn't have faith in his Texas Ranger brother because in her mind, Eli could also be connected to that phone call Eric had made a year ago.

Eli made a beeline toward them, glancing first at Jack before his attention lingered a moment on Caroline. Eli lifted an eyebrow. "You got your memory back, but you don't know who killed our father."

It wasn't a question. Nor was it especially sympathetic. But then, Eli wasn't known for his soft touch. His recent engagement had given him a sunnier outlook, but it didn't appear that he was going to spread any of that sunshine Caroline's way.

"I'm sorry," she said. "I wish I did know who killed him, because I would tell you. I also wish that I could trust you, but I don't."

Eli kept his attention on Caroline, studying her, before he shrugged. "Understood. But if you remember anything about me, you know I don't do things half-assed. If I'd actually helped Eric, I wouldn't have let a hostage overhear a conversation I'd had with him. A conversation that could have come back to bite me. That's just an FYI," he added in a growl before he turned back to Jack.

What Eli had said was true. He wasn't the sort to leave stones unturned or loose threads untied. Jack just wished his brother had tried to give Caroline a little more reassurance. She was already spooked, and none of them wanted her slipping into a panic mode.

But Caroline didn't panic. She simply nodded in response to Eli. So maybe that was progress. Soon, though, she'd need to trust all the Slater lawmen because they were her best shot at staying alive.

"I found the rental car," Eli threw out there, causing both Jack and Caroline to turn to him. "It was on an old ranch trail less than a mile from where you were attacked. No one was in it, but the CSIs will go through it."

Good. Finally, there was news that Jack wanted to hear. He hadn't expected the shooter to still be with the vehicle, but maybe the person had left fingerprints or trace evidence behind.

"There's a second set of fresh tire tracks on the trail," Eli went on. "Either the shooter had stashed another vehicle there so he could use it to getaway or else someone was waiting there for them."

A partner. Yeah. Jack had considered that,

too, though he was hoping the person was working alone.

"Can we get the model of the second vehicle from the tire tracks?" Jack asked.

"CSI will try, but it's the longest of long shots. They said it was a common tread."

Okay, so they likely wouldn't get much from that. Still, there was another angle on this. "Who rented that sedan?" Jack asked.

"Brad Smith," Eli immediately answered.

It was a common enough name, and judging from Caroline's headshake, it didn't ring any bells for her. Jack took out his phone to start a search on the man.

"Smith reserved the rental car online, but he had a valid credit card in that name," Eli went on. "It was one of those deals where Smith used a code the rental company gave him and used it to get the car from a specific spot on the lot."

"In other words, Smith didn't have face-to-face contact with a clerk," Jack concluded.

Eli confirmed that with a nod. "The rental company has security surveillance cameras in the lot where the vehicles are kept, and they've agreed to turn over the feed to us. They're emailing copies here and to the Ranger lab."

Jack was glad the rental car company was cooperating, but he was betting how this would play out. Smith—or whoever the hell he really was—likely knew there'd be cameras and had probably worn a disguise. Heck, a ball cap could have obscured his face. Still, they'd be able to get height and build, which in turn might give them something they could use against Kingston.

Well, it would if Smith matched Kingston's description.

"There's more," Eli said, and this time his tone had a darker edge to it. He made eye contact with Jack. "I had the Ranger lab do a deep run on all the Brad Smiths in the area, and something *interesting* came up."

"I'm listening," Jack grumbled when Eli hesitated.

And even with that prompt, Eli hesitated some more. A muscle jerked hard in his jaw. "Brad Smith was an alias that came up in an investigation a few years ago. Another sex-trafficking ring that wasn't connected to Dad's case. But according to the file notes, Smith was actually an undercover marshal."

Hell. Jack knew how this was about to play out, and he finished what Eli had been about to say. "Brad Smith is Lee Zeller."

Chapter Seven

Finally. That was Caroline's first reaction to what Jack had just said about Lee Zeller being Brad Smith.

That connection between Zeller and the rental car used in the attack brought together some of the pieces of this puzzle. She hadn't been wrong about overhearing Eric talk with someone in law enforcement. Or at least someone pretending to be in that line of work. But there would have been no pretense needed if Eric's conversation had indeed been with Zeller.

Jack turned to her, the questions all over his face, but Caroline didn't have the answers he wanted.

"No, I don't remember Eric ever mentioning Zeller's name," she volunteered. "But he didn't say any specific name during that phone call."

Plus, she'd been injured and drugged. She didn't want to bring that up now, though, because Jack and his brothers already had enough doubts as to what she'd overheard. She didn't want to add to those doubts and cause them to soften their attitudes about Zeller or any of their other fellow lawmen.

Jack made a sound to indicate he was thinking about this. "If Zeller did help Eric, if they were somehow connected to the sex-trafficking ring, then maybe Zeller thought you'd overheard something to incriminate him."

Maybe, and if so, that could be Zeller's motive to eliminate her. Still, there was something that didn't fit. "Why wouldn't Zeller have eliminated me sooner?" Caroline asked. "Or at least tried to do that? He's a marshal and could have easily gotten the location of the WITSEC house."

"Not easily," Jack insisted. "I'd put the location under several more layers of security, and if someone unauthorized had been poking around the files to find the address, the system should have alerted me."

"Still…" She shook her head. "Zeller probably could have managed it. So why wait to kill me?"

"As long as you didn't have your memory, you weren't a threat." Jack answered that so fast that it let her know he'd already reached that possible conclusion.

"But the timing doesn't fit," Caroline argued. "We were attacked only minutes after you learned I'd regained my memory. How would Zeller have…" She stopped when something occurred to her. "Zeller could have known about the computer searches I've done over the past few days. It wouldn't have been easy for him to do that, but if he'd been *keeping tabs* on me, he could have figured it out."

Both Jack and Eli nodded, causing the realization to settle hard in her stomach. Her searches could have been like loading a gun. Then, Zeller had pulled the trigger.

Well, maybe.

A possible motive was still a long way from proof that he'd committed a crime.

"You're sure when your father was investigating the sex trafficking that nothing incriminating came up about Zeller?" she asked.

Both Eli and Jack gave her flat looks. Of course, they were sure. They'd likely memorized everything about the case, and it had to eat away at both of them. Here it was their job to bring criminals to justice, and they hadn't been able to do that for their own father.

"It was more of a gut feeling," Jack said. "When Nicola's body turned up and my father had to investigate it, Zeller didn't want him involved. Part of me gets that. The sex ring was his case, but Zeller didn't even want to work with my dad. In fact, he tried everything to exclude him."

Caroline had worked with enough law enforcement officers, so she knew it wasn't unusual for one of them to feel that way and go all territorial. But in this case, it could be a red flag if Zeller hadn't wanted Sheriff Buck Slater digging into anything that would incriminate Zeller himself. However, it was just as possible that Jack and his brothers were being hypercritical. A sort of grabbing at straws in the hope that they could bring their father's killer to justice.

"And then there's Zeller's possible connection to the breach of security at your WITSEC house," Jack went on. "That gave me another bad feeling. Someone texted Kingston that address. Maybe Kingston himself, if he managed to hack into Justice Department files, but it could be someone else."

"Someone like Zeller," Caroline finished for him.

Jack nodded. "That's why I'm having Teagan go through the files to see who accessed that address."

"Maybe you don't trust Jack's partner, either?" Eli asked her after a long pause.

"Eric called a man that night," she quickly pointed out. But then Caroline had to pause, too. "Of course, that doesn't prove Teagan is clean, but I've got enough trouble without putting her under a microscope."

"Good point," Eli grumbled, and then he tipped his head to the computer on Kellan's desk. "You got access to that?" he asked Jack, checking the time. "If so, the surveillance footage from the car rental company should be ready."

"Yeah, I've got access," Jack said as if still in deep thought. *Troubled* thought, Caroline mentally corrected. Even though Jack didn't fully trust Zeller, it still had to be hard for him to think of a fellow marshal trying to murder them.

Caroline went to the computer when Jack did and she stood behind him, watching him work his way through the password and into Kellan's official emails. The file from the car rental company was there. When he clicked on it, Eli came to his side and all three of them focused on the monitor.

"It was an 8:00 a.m. pickup," Eli said, glancing at the notes on his phone.

Good. That would save them from watching hours of the feed. The timing also fit with something else—Zeller would have had plenty of time to get the car and drive out to Longview Ridge. For that matter, though, Kingston would have, too. Or any other suspect.

She watched as Jack fast-forwarded the images, but then he slowed to a normal speed when the figure came into view. A tall man who walked toward the black four-door sedan. And Caroline groaned at the same moment that Jack and Eli cursed.

The man was wearing a baseball cap, and he had on a bulky dark blue windbreaker with the collar turned up high on his neck. He kept his head down, the camera only getting a good shot of the hat and not the man's face. Worse, the build didn't help, either, because it appeared he'd stuffed things in his pants pockets, which could make him look heavier than he actually was.

Jack rewound the feed and went through it frame by frame until he stopped on the image that gave them a partial view of the guy's chin. Between the high collar and the shadow created by the ball cap, it wasn't very clear.

"That could be either Zeller or Kingston since they're about the same height," Jack grumbled under his breath.

Yes. Or someone either of them could have hired to get the car. "What about the handyman Zeller mentioned?" she asked. "Bennie Darnell. Can you pull up an ID on him?"

Jack didn't point out that it was a long shot. Even though it was. He just tapped into the

DMV files and accessed the man's photo and the details listed on his driver's license.

This time, all three of them cursed.

Because Bennie, too, had a similar height and weight to Zeller and Kingston. Not only were they not able to rule anyone out, but now they'd added another potential person of interest.

"Bennie has a record," Jack explained as he went through another database. "He was arrested for drug possession and driving under the influence ten years ago. He's been clean ever since."

Obviously, his record hadn't stopped him from getting a job, and Caroline doubted he'd been hired without some kind of background check. Still, it wouldn't hurt to do a deeper run on him. She was about to suggest that when Jack's phone rang, and she saw Zeller's name on the screen.

Eli must have seen it, too, because he muttered something about getting a cup of coffee, and he headed out of the office. Jack answered the call and put it on speaker.

"You wanted to talk to me?" Zeller snapped the moment he was on the line. He sounded annoyed, and Caroline bet his irritation would only increase after this chat.

Jack didn't waste any time responding. "Who knew about your alias, Brad Smith?"

Now there was some hesitation. "Why?" Zeller demanded.

"Because someone using that name rented the car used in the attack against Caroline and me."

She'd been right about the annoyance, but there was also some anger when Zeller belted out a string of profanities. "Someone's trying to set me up."

"Who knew that was your alias?" Jack pressed, speaking right over Zeller's cursing.

"Hell, anybody with access to our computers," Zeller spat out. "Anybody who came in contact with me when I was on an op and using that name."

"Narrow it down," Jack insisted. "Go through your case files and find someone who intersects with Caroline and me."

"Believe me, I will. Because I didn't have anything to do with that car or the attack. What about security cameras at the rental place?" Zeller quickly tacked on.

"I'm looking at it right now, and I can't rule you out."

"No, but you can sure as hell rule me out because I'm not a dirty marshal. Somebody's setting me up," Zeller repeated. "I want a copy of that surveillance feed. While you're getting that to me, I'll go through the files and get back to you." And with that, Zeller ended the call.

Caroline hadn't expected Zeller to just fess up to renting the car and then hiring someone to shoot at them. No. Even if he was as guilty as sin, Zeller wouldn't cop to anything because he'd know there wasn't any concrete evidence against him.

Not yet, anyway.

"I know the Ranger crime lab will try to enhance the security footage," she said, "but I'd like to have a go at it, too. I might be able to match the jawline to Bennie, Kingston or Zeller."

Jack didn't refuse her help, but he did look her straight in the eyes. A look that likely told him that she was exhausted. She also had a dull, throbbing headache. There'd been no time for her to calm down after the shooting. No chance for her to regain her footing. And the kiss hadn't helped with that. Maybe that was why Jack didn't come to her. Instead, he crammed his hands in the pockets of his jeans.

"As soon as Kellan finishes up with Kingston, we should be able to leave for another safe house," he said.

Her first response was relief. She could get some quiet time and try to level out her nerves. But another concern popped up immediately. For her to get to a safe house, she'd have to leave the sheriff's office and go outside, where their attacker could be lying in wait for them. It was a risk. Then again, she couldn't stay here amid all the badges that she wasn't sure she could trust.

So this was the rock and the hard place.

"Where's the safe house?" she asked.

Jack didn't get a chance to answer her, though, because Eli stepped back into the doorway. "You've got a visitor," Eli said, shifting his gaze to both Jack and her.

Instant alarm went through Caroline. Jack seemed to stiffen with attention. He immediately stepped in front of her.

"Who is it?" Jack pressed.

"Lily Terrell," Eli answered. "She says you'll want to see her because she believes she's a suspect in today's attack."

WELL, JACK HADN'T seen this coming. In fact, he'd thought he was going to have to contact Lily to let her know that he had some questions for her. He'd expected an heiress like that to give him some flak. Instead, here she was, walking straight toward Kellan's office.

Jack closed the laptop and checked to make sure there was nothing that a person of interest shouldn't be seeing. There wasn't. Well, nothing other than Caroline. Jack didn't care for the fact that she was going to have to face yet someone else who may have had a part in the attack.

"She's not armed," Eli told Jack.

Jack appreciated that his brother had frisked the woman, but after getting a good look at her, he figured there weren't many places Lily could have hidden a weapon. She was a tall woman, close to six feet, and she was rail thin. The cobalt blue dress she was wearing clung to every inch of her. No chance of her hiding much in the tiny hand-sized purse she was holding.

"Marshal Slater," she greeted, her voice a sultry drawl. It went well with her cool violet eyes and the auburn hair that tumbled over her shoulders.

She flashed him a smile, extending it to Eli and then to Caroline. "Miss Moser," Lily added.

"How do you know me?" Caroline asked, taking the question right out of Jack's mouth.

"I'm familiar with your work on Crime-Track that you did at the university with Gemma Hanson." Lily's answer was quick and unruffled. Actually, *unruffled* was a good description for the woman herself. If she was bothered by being considered a suspect, she didn't show it.

Caroline had indeed worked on that project, and Jack figured that was common knowledge. The media had hashed and rehashed it after one of the research assistants on the project, Eric Lang, had been uncovered as a serial killer.

"It's work you should continue," Lily added

to Caroline a moment later. "It could be very beneficial to law enforcement agencies."

Caroline lifted an eyebrow. "I doubt anyone wants to trust a profiler who worked side by side with a serial killer and didn't know it."

Lily made a sound that could have meant anything and turned back to Jack. "The shooting was on the news," she said. "Details were sketchy, but when I heard your name and Caroline's, I thought it best if I came in."

"And why is that?" Jack had no intention of showing his hand until he found out more about this visit.

"Bennie Darnell is a handyman at New Beginnings, and he told me about Marshal Lee Zeller's *interest* in me. When I heard about the attack on the news, I assumed Zeller would be trying to convince you that I was somehow involved. So I came here to clear my name."

Jack exchanged glances with Caroline and saw that she was just as surprised as he was. Zeller had made it seem as if Bennie was his mole, but obviously the handyman still had some loyalty to his employer. In turn, that called into question any info that Bennie had given Zeller, because maybe Bennie was just the sort who liked to tell people whatever it was they wanted to hear.

"Why exactly does Marshal Zeller have an

interest in you?" Jack asked. He tried to keep his tone level, more of a request than a demand, since he was still trying to figure out if Lily was playing some kind of game or if she truly was concerned about making sure her name was clean.

"Because of Skylar Greer." She didn't hesitate, and Lily looked him straight in the eyes when she spoke. Then she dragged in a long breath. "Even though he's never come right out and said it, Marshal Zeller seems to believe I had some part in Skylar leaving New Beginnings. I didn't."

Interesting that Lily had used the word "leaving" when Zeller had described it as a disappearance.

"Why did the woman *leave*?" Jack pressed.

Now she dodged his gaze, but only for a few seconds. "I'm not sure. She didn't speak to me about it, but I assume Skylar felt as if there was some other place she wanted to be. Hopefully, a safe place," she softly added.

Yeah, Jack hoped the same thing, and also wished he could know for sure that the woman was actually alive. "You think Skylar could have gotten lured back into sex trafficking?"

Lily didn't jump to deny that, and she glanced at Caroline. "You both know how hard it is to come back from a traumatic situation. Skylar was a troubled young woman and didn't trust easily. I think it would be very easy for her to slip back into her old ways."

Lily's words were right. So was the concerned expression on her face. But something in her voice and body language didn't ring true for Jack. Or maybe he was just projecting because of the sliver of doubt that Zeller had put in his head.

"Skylar didn't trust you?" Caroline came out and asked.

"Sadly, no," Lily answered.

Again, right tone, but it did nothing to ease that bad feeling. He considered a moment how to deal with this and went with the direct approach.

"I want copies of Skylar's records," Jack insisted.

Lily's expression never changed, and she didn't even pause. "I'm afraid I'll have to insist you get a warrant for that. The privacy of the residents is a top priority for me."

It was the exact answer he'd expected from the woman. Maybe stonewalling. Maybe just trying to be ethical. "I'll get the warrant, and then you'll need to come back in here to give me an official statement."

Lily nodded, but some wariness crept into

her eyes. "It sounds as if I'll need my lawyer for that."

"That's probably a good idea." Jack didn't especially want to deal with her lawyer, but he liked that his comment had caused her some tension. He wanted Lily out of her comfort zone, since nervous suspects were more likely to make mistakes.

"We'll get into this more after I have the warrant," Jack continued, and he decided to go with a long shot. "Tell me about your relationship with Eric."

Lily's eyes widened, and she fired nervous glances at Caroline, Eli and him. "There was no relationship." Her voice was clipped now. "I knew Eric only because we were in the same social circles."

"You knew him," Jack emphasized.

Lily's mouth tightened for a moment. "Eric and I rarely spoke and only at parties and such."

But the bottom line was that she had indeed known him, and Jack was fairly certain that hadn't come up in the investigation. Of course, there would have been no reason for it to have. Lily hadn't been a suspect, and there'd been no record of Eric ever contacting her. The only reason Jack had asked her about it was because he was toying with the idea that Eric and Zeller might have had some part in the sex trafficking.

They could have teamed up to lure Buck to that inn so Zeller could kill him.

That was a long shot.

However, if Eric and Zeller were connected, then maybe Lily was, too. That could explain why Zeller was so hell-bent on pinning something illegal on her. Maybe he wanted her to be put away so she couldn't expose his own crimes.

"What about Kingston Morris?" Jack went on. "You know him, too?"

Lily's slow nod was as uncertain as the rest of her. "Yes. Again, the same circles, and I knew him slightly more than Eric. How is he involved in this?" she asked.

Jack knew it wouldn't be long before word got out, so he decided to tell Lily so he could see her reaction. "Kingston showed up at Caroline's house. Trespassing," he added. "Her address was protected and wasn't easily accessible. Still, Kingston managed to get it, and shortly afterward, Caroline was attacked."

Lily pressed her hand to her chest as if to steady her heart. "You suspect Kingston of trying to kill her?"

"He's being interviewed now," Jack answered, dodging Lily's direct question, and yeah, Kingston was a suspect all right.

"I see." Some of the color drained from Lily's face. She paused, moistened her lips. "Is it because of Grace Wainwright? Is that how Kingston got Caroline's address?"

Jack glanced at Caroline to see if she recognized the name, but she only shook her head.

"Who's Grace Wainwright?" Jack asked.

Lily opened her mouth, then closed it just as fast. Maybe rethinking what she'd been about to say. "Grace was at New Beginnings. She had gotten caught up in sex trafficking," Lily added. "She also had some family problems that prevented her from going home, and she asked if she could stay there while she straightened out her life. However, before that, she was romantically involved with Kingston."

For someone who was hesitant to share much on Skylar, Lily clearly didn't feel the need to hold back with Grace.

Jack stared at Lily. "And why would Grace have known Caroline's address?"

"Because Grace has excellent computer skills and wasn't always ethical about whose information she accessed. She could have hacked into the files, found Caroline's address and given it to Kingston. Or sold it to him."

Jack didn't have trouble latching on to what Lily hadn't said. "Grace accessed information about you?"

Lily's mouth tightened. "She did. Actually, she managed to steal some funds from my bank account. When I caught her, I told her she had to leave New Beginnings. She did, but I've since heard rumors that she's still using her talents for illegal activities."

He was definitely going to have to question Grace about that. But if she had indeed managed to get into Justice Department files, then she had to be better than just "excellent" when it came to hacking.

Jack made a mental note to contact Grace ASAP, and then he moved on to the next question he had for Lily. "Why is Zeller so hell-bent about coming after you?"

Lily hesitated, and he saw the pulse kick up on her throat. "I suspect it's because he feels guilty." She stopped, huffed. "Look, I'm guessing you're not going to want to hear anything negative about one of your fellow marshals…"

"Trust me, I want to hear it," Jack insisted.

Lily nodded and made a suit-yourself sound. "From what I've gathered from conversations with some of the girls who came to New Beginnings, I believe Zeller knew Nicola Gunderson and that he talked her into helping him bring down the sex-trafficking ring."

Everything inside Jack went still. He definitely hadn't heard Zeller mention knowing the dead girl, and he was pretty sure that should have come out by now. Especially since it was his father who was investigating her murder.

"I'm not surprised Zeller didn't mention any of this to you," Lily went on. "In fact, I suspect he doesn't want anyone to know that he's the reason that Nicola was murdered."

Chapter Eight

Caroline watched as Jack located Grace's number and tried to call the woman. No answer. But maybe she'd call back soon. And perhaps Grace wouldn't try to avoid them simply because she didn't want to be questioned about her possible involvement in the attack.

Of course, if Grace was indeed avoiding them, it likely wasn't because Lily had warned her. Not enough time for that. It had only been a couple of minutes since she'd left the sheriff's office. Plus, why would Lily have volunteered the woman's name if she was just going to go and warn her?

Jack left Grace a message for her to call him and then tried Zeller again. Even though he hadn't put his phone on speaker, Caroline was close enough that she heard the call to Zeller go straight to voice mail.

Unlike Grace, Zeller was someone who could absolutely be avoiding them.

If what Lily had said was true about Zeller coaxing Nicola into helping him, then the marshal should have already spilled that. Not just to Jack's father but to Jack and his siblings. Zeller definitely needed to answer some questions, and with each new bit of information, Caroline was trusting him less and less.

Jack shook his head in frustration over not getting through to Zeller before he fired off a text to someone, and then he looked at her. Whatever he saw on her face caused his frustration to worsen. "You're exhausted," he concluded. "I'm sorry. I should have already gotten you out of here."

"No, you shouldn't have," she argued. "You needed to be here so you can find the person who tried to kill us."

And while things were still unsettled between them, Caroline knew one thing for certain. She didn't want Jack sending her off with anyone else. Especially anyone else with a badge.

Even though touching him was playing with fire, Caroline risked sliding her hand down his arm. A gesture meant to comfort him, along with getting some comfort for herself. Jack was the only person who could soothe her like this.

Now his eyes flashed with a different emotion. Heat layered over the irritation of the stalled investigation, and soon even the worry seemed to fade away. Apparently, she also had a soothing effect on him, and it was effective if she didn't count the whole arousal thing.

Caroline figured that Jack counted it.

Neither of them had time to act on it, though, because of the approaching footsteps. That sound caused them to move apart, and Jack shook his head as if to clear it before he stepped in front of her. Preparing for a threat. But he relaxed some when Kellan appeared in the doorway. Kingston was right behind him.

"Am I done here now?" Kingston asked. He didn't sound smug or cooperative now, which meant Kellan had grilled him hard. Good. Maybe Kellan had also gotten some info they could use.

"No, you're not done," Jack snapped. He shifted his attention to Kellan. "Lily Terrell came in and chatted with us. She'll be back later with her lawyer for an official interview, but for now she had some interesting theories. One that's connected to Kingston."

Kingston groaned. "Did Lily accuse me of something, too?"

"Do you know Grace Wainwright?" Jack went on, ignoring Kingston's question.

Kingston blinked, clearly surprised by the topic. "Of course, I know her. We were once lovers."

Jack didn't pause even a second. "Did she get you Caroline's address?"

"No." Kingston looked ready to gear up with a more detailed, angrier denial, but then he stopped. "Maybe. But if she did, she didn't tell me she was the one who texted it to me."

No, because that would have incriminated her in a felony. Of course, it was possible Grace had given him the address and that he was covering for her. Caroline figured Jack would be digging deep into the woman's background to try to determine that.

Kellan waited until Jack gave him the go-ahead nod before he turned to Kingston. "You can go, *for now*, but don't leave the state. I'll be bringing you back in when I have more info."

That clearly didn't please Kingston, but he didn't waste any time arguing with them. He turned and hurried out.

"Lily thinks Zeller knew Nicola," Jack told his brother when Kingston was out of earshot. "He might have even talked Nicola into helping him break up the sex-trafficking ring."

The muscles tightened in Kellan's face. "I'll make some calls and see what I can find out." He glanced away and cursed. "We're not getting answers, just a whole bunch of questions."

"Yeah," Jack agreed, the fatigue now back in his voice. "I've already requested authorization to look into Zeller's computer. That might get us something."

It would, unless Zeller had already wiped the hard drive. Or disposed of it. For someone with the right skills, there were plenty of ways to erase data.

"I also need a warrant to get into the records at New Beginnings," Jack added. "I want to have a look at the file of a woman that Zeller says went missing. But I can wait a little while on that. For now, I need to go ahead and get Caroline out of here. You think you can spare a deputy until morning, or should I see if Teagan can help?"

Kellan glanced at Caroline and then out into the bullpen. "Since Caroline seems to be more comfortable with female officers, why don't you take Raylene. Caroline knows her."

Yes, she did. Deputy Raylene McNeal. Caroline didn't like putting trust in a person simply because of their gender, but in this case it helped her relax a little. Well, relax about who'd be doing bodyguard duty for her, but her nerves went zinging again when she realized they'd be going back outside.

Kellan stepped into the squad room, motioning for Raylene, and a moment later, the sturdy-looking brunette deputy joined him in the doorway, where Kellan, Jack and she had a whispered conversation. Something that Jack said had Kellan frowning and groaning, but Jack persisted and finished whatever point he was making.

When they'd finished talking, Raylene glanced at Caroline in a gesture that was probably meant to reassure her. Surprisingly, it did. Caroline hated that she needed to be babysat like this, but she wasn't stupid. She'd come close to dying too many times to take unnecessary risks by turning down protection.

"Caroline, Raylene and I will go in a cruiser," Jack explained. "Gunnar will follow as backup but will come back here once he's sure it's safe. Raylene will stay with us."

Raylene nodded. "Just let me get the overnight bag I keep in my locker."

While Kellan spoke to Gunnar, Raylene hurried toward the break room. The deputy didn't take long and was back in under a minute. That was still plenty enough time for Caroline's stomach to start churning with the reminder that the person who'd tried to kill them could be waiting outside.

"Move fast," Jack instructed, and he hooked his arm around Caroline's waist to get her moving.

There were two cruisers parked out front. Raylene and Gunnar went out first, each of them hurrying to get behind the wheel of their respective vehicle. Jack had one last look around before he moved with Caroline, and the moment they were inside the cruiser, Raylene took off with Gunnar following right behind her.

Jack continued to keep watch. So did Caroline. She studied each person on Main Street as if they were a would-be gunman, but no one attempted to fire at them. That still didn't make her relax. She kept her eyes on their surroundings, wishing that she had a gun so she could defend herself if it came down to it.

Raylene drove out of town and onto the rural road that snaked through the countryside. There were no pedestrians here to watch, only miles of woods and pastures, and it didn't take Caroline long to realize where they were going. She whirled toward Jack so fast that her neck popped.

"You're taking me to your family's ranch," she blurted out, and was certain her tone and expression let him know she didn't like that.

"Actually, I'm taking you to my place, but as I'm sure you remember, it's on the ranch."

Oh, yes. She remembered all right. It was the wood-and-stone house where she'd spent many nights with Jack. As his lover. And while it might be more comfortable than standing around at the sheriff's office, it wasn't exactly "safe." Not with all the memories the place held. Specifically memories of Jack and her in bed.

"You can't think going there is a good idea," Caroline said.

He shrugged and continued to keep watch. "I have a security system, and the ranch hands will help guard the place."

Again, that didn't make it safe.

"Are all the repairs done?" Raylene asked him, her gaze briefly meeting Jack's in the rear-view mirror.

"They are. The damage wasn't that bad."

Caroline didn't need clarification on the repairs or damage because she'd heard about the *incident* that'd happened at his place. Someone who'd been after Jack's brother, Owen, had rammed his car into the porch. She'd heard bits and pieces about it from Lucille and the media reports she'd accessed, but Caroline figured she hadn't gotten the full story. Wasn't sure she wanted it, either. She had enough bad stuff in her head without adding more.

"Considering that an attack happened so recently at your place, maybe we should take that as some kind of sign not to go there," Caroline grumbled.

"The attack caused me to beef up security," Jack said as if that answered all of her concerns. It didn't. But then Caroline didn't know anywhere they could go where she wouldn't feel the danger looming over her.

Still…

She had to put her argument on hold for a moment when Raylene pulled to a stop in front of Jack's. Despite those repairs and the security upgrade that he'd mentioned, the place looked exactly the same. It definitely wasn't sprawling like the main house just up the road, where Kellan lived and helped run the family ranch. Jack's place only had three bedrooms and two baths, and was as comfortable-looking and laid-back as the owner.

"Wait here a sec," Jack told her.

He got out and ran to the front door. Caroline watched as he unlocked it and then used his phone to disengage the security system. He also went in, likely to search the place, before he came back out. As they'd done at the sheriff's office, they moved fast, and only after Jack had Raylene and her inside did he motion for Gunnar to leave.

While Jack reset the security alarms, Caroline walked into the living room and glanced around. No changes here, either, and that included the two framed photos of Jack and her on the mantel. In one, he had his arm crooked playfully around her, his mouth pressed to her cheek, while she had a huge grin on her face. The other photo was a shot of Kellan and Gemma standing next to Jack and her, all of them smiling. Obviously, they were taken in much happier times.

"You can take the guest room," Jack told Raylene, and he motioned toward the first room off the hall.

With her overnight bag in hand, Raylene headed in that direction, leaving Caroline with Jack.

"I'll take the couch. You can use my room," he added to Caroline, holding her hand to take her there.

She knew the way, every step of it, and every scent was familiar because it was Jack's. By the time she walked into the bedroom suite, her body was humming with that familiarity. With those memories of what had gone on here. None of the bad stuff. Not here. This was all warmth and pleasure.

He'd kept the same quilt, and Caroline knew the feel of it. The soft cotton that had slid against her skin every time she'd been naked in that bed.

"Afraid to be alone with me?" he asked, coming up behind her.

She shook her head. "Fear isn't the right word for it—"

"You told me you loved me," he interrupted.

"That morning before Eric took you, you told me that."

No need for him to clarify which morning, but she didn't like his timing in bringing it up now. "I remember." She cleared her throat so it would have some sound, and had to do it again. Great. Her throat was clogged now, and her breathing wasn't faring much better.

Jack moved in front of her, studying her face. He wasn't frowning, but it was close. "You don't feel the same way about me now."

She wanted to groan. Apparently, he wasn't content with just having her surrounded by old memories of them as a couple. He wanted her to relive it with words, too. And it was working. She felt the slow hum of heat circle around her.

"I'm not sure what I feel," Caroline settled for saying, but it required another throat clearing.

Her answer didn't smooth his near frown. But it was partly true. She didn't know about still being in love. She'd had no time to sort out her feelings, but when it came to Jack, she was certain about plenty of other things. She wanted him more than her next heartbeat. More than she wanted to feel strong and whole again.

And that want was quickly turning into a need.

The silence vibrated between them as he stared at her. It ended when Jack cursed. "I considered offering you no-strings-attached sex. Just to burn off this heat so we could possibly think about something else. *Anything* else. But I can't do that."

Silence fell again, this time because he'd stunned her. "You can't have sex?" And she hated the disappointment in her voice.

A flicker of annoyance, and heat, went through his eyes. "I can't give you the no-strings. The sex is going to happen, but not until you know that it won't be just to satisfy some raw animal urges. *Strings*," he repeated, emphasizing it. "I'll want that I-love-you from you again. Maybe not tonight, but I'll want it soon."

Caroline was about to remind him that he'd never given her those words, but Jack snapped her to him and kissed her. It was hard and rough, not just his mouth but the grip he had on her arms. The roughness was something that Caroline quickly realized made it even better. He wasn't going to treat her like glass. The fragile kind of glass that broke with a careless touch.

He was going to break her in a whole different way. And there'd be nothing careless about it.

Cupping the back of her neck, Jack deepened the kiss. The physical part of it, anyway, since the emotional part was already as deep as it could get. Or so Caroline thought. He proved her wrong when he stopped and eased back enough to stare into her eyes.

There it was. The face that could have been created for an ancient god. The pretty ones who could be both ruthless and very, very desirable. His eyes, dark. That rumpled black hair. Oh, and that scent. Leather and male. It seeped into her, mingling with the heat that his kiss had already flamed.

Jack waited a heartbeat, maybe giving her a chance to change her mind, all the while knowing that she wouldn't do that. Caroline knew it, too.

The next kiss was just a brush of his mouth over hers. Slow and sensual with their breaths mingling. And he looked at her again. Gauging her reaction. She was breathing too fast, and her pulse was at a full gallop. Every inch of her was quivering, waiting, and she didn't want the wait to continue for even a second longer.

She didn't have to.

Jack took her mouth again, and there it was. The raw animal urge that went to full flame and beyond when his hand slid underneath her dress and straight into her panties. Caroline made a gasp of pleasure when he plunged his fingers into her. So much pleasure that his touch would have brought her to a fast climax if he hadn't suddenly stopped.

"No. It won't be that easy," he said, his voice as intense as the look he gave her. Jack reached behind her, shut the door and locked it. "It'll never be that easy between us."

It sounded a little like a threat, and he hooked his arm around her, lifting her as if she weighed nothing. Those strong, corded arms closed around her. He kissed her, hard and deep again, while he took her to his bed. He practically dumped her on the too-soft mattress that swelled up around her.

When he didn't immediately join her, she reached for him, only to realize that his plan was to stay standing so he could strip off her dress.

Which he did.

Jack sent it flying. Then he got on the bed, his knee landing between her legs. As he loomed over her, she could feel his jeans rub against the inside of her thighs. Could hear the rough rhythm of his breath.

He kissed her breasts through her bra. Again, not gently. Both his hands and his mouth were rough as he yanked off her panties and then her bra. He'd said he hadn't wanted easy, whatever that meant, but he apparently wanted fast.

Good.

Because she wanted that, too. Fast meant she didn't have to think about this. For that to happen, she needed him as naked as he'd just gotten her. Caroline went after the buttons on his shirt, but when he took her nipple into his mouth, the heat roared through her. Fingers to toes and every single place in between. She gave up on the shirt and went after his zipper instead.

Jack didn't stop her when she freed him from his jeans and boxers, but he did stop the maddening kisses. Again, their gazes met. And held. Just as he plunged into her.

Caroline made another of those gasps. Pleasure, yes. Definitely that. Mixed with the brief shock of his hard thrust. Then, even more pleasure. So much more.

This was the animal urge part. His eyes held a need of a different kind, though. The pretty, ruthless god planned to claim what he believed to be already his. To possess her. It frightened her a little to think that he could do just that. Frightened her even more that she wanted him to do it.

It didn't take much. A few more of those deep, plundering strokes inside her, and Caroline couldn't have held back the climax even if she'd wanted to. She didn't. But she refused to go falling over that edge alone.

Knowing exactly how to undo him, she lifted her hips, clamping her knees around him and dragging him harder into her. She let the muscles in her body force him into joining her. Her vision blurred, but still she watched him. And he watched her...while they fell together.

Caroline could feel those strings tightening around her, and while Jack gathered her into his arms and kissed her, she prayed for so many things. That this wouldn't be the mistake she was certain it was. Because those strings weren't just about love and broken hearts. They were about priority and focus.

And those strings could get them both killed.

Chapter Nine

Caroline still slept like a rock. Jack now had proof that it was something about her that hadn't changed. Facedown, arms outstretched and butt naked on his bed, she'd slept all night and then through the beep of his morning alarm. Ditto for staying sacked out during his shower and the phone calls he'd gotten and the ones that he'd made.

While Jack would have liked to let her sleep even longer, he had things to do that couldn't wait. So he poured a huge mug of black coffee that he'd brewed strong enough to the point of being bitter. Just the way Caroline liked it. He added a single ice cube to it to cool it down enough for her to drink it fast—which she would do.

When he went back into the bedroom, he had to push aside the punch of attraction he got from seeing her in his bed. The attraction got another punch when he recalled in perfect detail all the things they'd done there.

Oh, man.

He really needed to figure out a way to deal with what he felt for her so he could do everything possible to keep her out of danger. That had to be his mission now because he couldn't lose her again.

She stirred the moment Jack held the mug near her nose, and then he moved it so her flailing hands wouldn't knock into it and spill it. Yawning and groaning at the same time, she lumbered to a sitting position and groped to take the coffee. Jack kept hold of it, too, until he was certain of her grip.

No sips for her. As expected, she downed several long gulps as if it were the cure for all ills, before she looked up as if just realizing he was there. She smiled until her attention landed on his clothes.

"You're dressed," she said, frowning now.

"Been up for a while." Jack eased down on the bed next to her, but not too close. If he touched her, he'd be toast. "You need to slap me. I forgot to use a condom last night."

"Uh." Caroline repeated that sound, pushed her hair from her face. "I'm on the pill. I started it last month to regulate my periods." She added that last part in a barely audible mumble, and continued, "I haven't been with anyone since, well, just since."

Judging from the way her face flushed, that seemed to embarrass her. Ironic, since she was stark naked.

Something his body had noticed, of course.

Actually, what his body wanted to do was get back in that bed with her and go for another round or two. Not going to happen, though. But the comment that embarrassed her pleased him more than it should have. Which was stupid. Because the reason she hadn't been with anyone else was because she'd been hurt and not because of some unremembered commitment to him.

"Zeller still hasn't returned my calls, but Kellan texted me," Jack explained, forcing his mind back where it belonged, and it darn sure shouldn't be on her breasts. "The warrant came through on the missing girl from New Beginnings, and we have the file. Lily Terrell's coming into the sheriff's office with her lawyer in—" he checked his watch "—about an hour."

"An hour," she repeated, and she sounded a little panicked now.

"I'd like to be there to hear what Lily has to say about those files," Jack went on, "and I don't want you here alone. Raylene's already gone home, but Gunnar's her relief, and he's waiting out front in a cruiser to take us in."

That got Caroline scrambling off the bed and into his bathroom. Gulping down coffee and mumbling, she turned on the shower. What she didn't do was shut the door, so he got even more of the drive-Jack-crazy peep show of her naked body behind the clear glass of the shower stall.

"I had your other things brought over from the WITSEC house," he called out to her. "They're in a suitcase next to the vanity."

While she showered, Jack gathered up what little willpower he had left and went back into the kitchen to finish his own coffee. He then phoned Teagan. It was his second call to her that morning. The first one had been an hour ago, so maybe she had something on how the location of the WITSEC house had been breached.

"You're not going to like what I'm about to tell you," Teagan said the moment she answered, and that caused Jack to groan.

"What happened?" he snapped, trying to steel himself for what would be bad news.

"All the WITSEC files are intact. None of them have been tampered with." She didn't snap at him, but there was irritation in her voice that let him know he might have preferred that to whatever else she was about to tell him. "I think the breach came from the laptop Caroline was using, the one you had couriered to me. Did you know she has hacking skills?" Teagan tacked on to that without even pausing.

"Yeah. One of her many talents," he grumbled. Along with picking locks, hot-wiring cars and driving him crazy. "There were filters on that laptop," Jack pointed out.

"Caroline got past them, and because her skills are better than ours, it took the geeks all night to find it. Several of the sites she used to do a search on Eric Lang had a tracker on them. Something experimental and beyond my skill set to explain. It's called Geo-Trace. It wouldn't have alerted her, and it was well hidden in the website codes. But the geeks think that's how someone found her."

Jack cursed, not just because he was pissed about the hacking but because this could crush Caroline. This could put her on the fast track to a panic attack and a guilt trip. Hell, she'd want to be offering to take a bullet for him because she would see this as having put him in danger.

"If it works the way the geeks think it does," Teagan explained, "Geo-Trace would have allowed someone to track the computer without getting a warrant. And Caroline wouldn't have known about the risk. Like I said, Geo-Trace is still in the experimental stages. Whoever put it on the sites was probably looking for her."

And had found her.

"See if the geeks can figure out who put Geo-Trace on the sites," he suggested. "Maybe try a reverse hacking maneuver." Ironically, it was something Caroline might be able to do, but he didn't want to go to her with this just yet.

"I'll try, but the Geo-Trace program corrupted itself when our techs tried to examine it. They got portions of it, but it was as if it had an encoded virus to stop someone from digging into it too much."

A fail-safe. One that would have required some serious computer skills. That still didn't convince him to bring this to Caroline. Even if he caught flak for it later, which he was certain he would.

"Don't mention this to Caroline," he added to Teagan.

Teagan rattled off a string of profanities before she said, "You're not going to question her about it?"

"Not right now. I need to ease her into it so that it doesn't send her into a tailspin."

Teagan groaned. "What part of your body are you thinking with right now?"

"Probably the wrong one," he admitted and ended the call just as Caroline hurried into the room.

She was dressed, mostly, but still adjusting

the above-the-knee denim skirt and snug red top. Clothes that hugged curves on Caroline that he wished he couldn't see right now.

Yeah, the wrong part of his body was doing the thinking, and that had to stop. With the breach of the WITSEC location, it wasn't a stretch for someone to figure out that she would have gone with him. That was why he hurried when he got her out of the house and into the cruiser. He had to concentrate on who had attacked them and stop the person from coming after them again.

Jack frowned when he looked up at the sky. The iron gray clouds were already moving on, indicating a storm was on the way. He didn't mind bad weather, but he didn't like the idea of it happening when he was trying to get Caroline back and forth from the sheriff's office.

Gunnar flashed Caroline a grin that he seemed to cut short when Jack scowled at him. He knew that Gunnar didn't have any romantic interest in Caroline. He was just being friendly, but Jack wanted the deputy in concentration mode, too.

"Did they find the shooter?" Caroline asked.

"No. The CSI team processed the car, and all the prints, fibers and trace they collected were sent to the lab. They might find something," Jack tried to assure her.

Since she'd been a criminal profiler and had dealt with investigations for years, Caroline probably knew that was a long shot. Anything collected from a rental car wouldn't necessarily belong to the last person who'd been inside it. Plus, a would-be killer had likely made sure not to leave any evidence behind.

Caroline shifted in the seat and studied him. "Is something wrong? I mean, something other than the obvious?"

There were two kinds of obvious here. The investigation and the personal. Jack had filled her in on everything about the case except for the likelihood that her laptop had been the reason her location was compromised. He still intended to hold off on asking her about that, which left them with the personal. And yes, there were things about that they also hadn't touched on yet.

Since Gunnar was only a few feet away, Jack reminded himself to keep his voice low. "I'm worried I messed up things last night."

Caroline stared at him, her expression flat. "I'm guessing you're not talking about the sex itself but rather the distraction it caused."

He nodded. Neither of them was going to dispute that the sex had been good. Darn good. Heck, they couldn't even try to pretend that it wouldn't happen again. But in this case, there could be a price to pay.

"You're on fragile ground," he said. "I know that. You're recovering from a nightmare that hasn't ended yet." And now he had to pause and figure out how to sort out the jumble of thoughts and emotions going through his mind. It'd been too long without her, and the need had been too much to overcome. "I'm sorry if this is messing with your head."

Her eyebrow rose, and for a moment he saw the flash of humor. Jack almost expected her to make a joke, something along the lines of it hadn't been her head he'd been messing with. But the humor faded as quickly as it had come.

"I suspect it messed with your head, too," she said. "What I don't want it to do is make you feel that you have to shelter me." But Caroline immediately waved that off. "I'm not talking about protective custody here. I'm not stupid. I need that. I need you."

Jack hated that the needing-him part made him feel a lot better than it should have.

She huffed and moved closer, the side of her arm sliding against his chest as she shifted in the seat. Caroline looked him straight in the eyes. "I want you to treat me the way you did in bed," she whispered. "I didn't feel damaged or broken then. And even if I am both of those things, I don't want you to make me feel as if I am. Understand?"

Oh, yeah. He understood all right. It'd been the heat that had caused him to take her hard and fast. No kid gloves. But the bottom line was that while she was healing, she was indeed still broken, and Jack had no intentions of adding to that. It meant he'd walk a fine line between his feelings for her and his need to protect her. Thankfully, he didn't have to get into the details of how he'd manage that, because Gunnar pulled to a stop in front of the sheriff's office.

Caroline's eyes met his again as if she wanted to delay getting out until he gave her some kind of assurance, but Gunnar remedied that, as well, by hurrying to open the door to the building for them. Clearly, the deputy was standing guard and waiting for them to go inside. On Caroline's huff and Jack's sigh of relief, that was exactly what they did.

As he'd done on their previous visit, Jack didn't linger around. He took Caroline past the noise and chatter in the squad room and into Kellan's office. His brother was there at his desk and working on his laptop. Gunnar peeled off from them and went to his desk.

"Lily's already here," Kellan told them, his eyes still on his laptop. "She's in the interview room with her lawyer." He finally looked up from his computer and his attention landed on Jack. Then on Caroline. "You two look…"

"Think carefully about how to finish that," Jack warned him. He wasn't in the mood for another lecture after he'd already gotten a scolding from Teagan.

"You look slightly more relaxed than you did yesterday," Kellan finished after a pause. "It won't last. Lily's not happy about you getting those warrants, so she came in here ranting."

A surprise, since Lily hadn't reached the ranting stage the day before. But then maybe the woman hadn't thought Jack would actually get the warrant.

"Here's the file on Skylar." Kellan turned his laptop in their direction. "There supposedly isn't a hard copy, only the digital one."

Lily was going to have to wait, because Jack wanted a look at this before he spoke to her. "Anything about the file jump out at you?" Jack asked Kellan as he pulled up Skylar's record.

But before Kellan could even respond, Jack saw an immediate problem. The file was too short. Two pages. The first was an intake form with basic stuff like name, age and next of kin. The next was a record of places the woman had been sent for job interviews.

"There are no reports from counselors or such," Jack concluded.

Kellan made a sound of agreement. "There's nothing about room assignments, day-to-day chores or any interaction with staff." He shook his head in disgust. "I've asked the computer guys at the Ranger lab to go through the files and see if anything was deleted in the past twenty-four hours. If so, we can look into charging Lily with obstruction of justice."

Was Lily really that stupid as to try to hide info from them? Maybe. People did dumb things all the time.

Caroline reached around Jack and typed something on the keyboard while her gaze skirted over the screen. "The file was modified nine hours ago."

That would have been just before the warrant had been served.

"I can't tell if anything was deleted," Caroline went on, "but the file was created a little over a year ago, and that fits the timing for when the woman would have arrived at New Beginnings." She continued to study the screen. "For only two pages, someone certainly spent a lot of time in this file. Over twenty-five hours."

That was too much for simply logging job interviews and background. Still, it wasn't proof of a crime. "Lily's lawyers could maybe say that the file was just left open and that's why the time doesn't jive with the amount of info that'd been entered."

"I want to talk to some of the other women at New Beginnings," Kellan said. "I'll find out if they've had counseling or anything else since they've been staying there. It might help if I also talk to previous residents and find out why Skylar left."

That was a necessary step, one of those drone-work chores that cops had to do in the hope of finding threads they could tug. It could give them something they could use against Lily, but it would take time.

"Does your warrant cover the computers at New Beginnings?" Caroline asked. "Because if so, I could get you what you need this morning so you wouldn't have to wait for the crime lab."

Kellan shook his head. "It only covers the one file." Then he paused. "But I'll see what I can do about getting another warrant so we can search through any-and everything in the damn building."

He took out his phone and stepped to the side to make the call, but he stopped when the front door opened. Kellan's grunt of irritation caused Jack's attention to zoom in that direction.

Zeller walked into the building.

"If you deal with him, I can get started on that warrant," Kellan said, and when Jack nodded, his brother went out into the bullpen to make the call.

"Don't start giving me grief about why I haven't returned your calls," Zeller griped the moment he stepped into Kellan's office. "I've been tied up on an investigation in Austin."

Jack didn't know about any such investigation, but it'd be easy enough to check. Which probably meant Zeller was telling the truth. Or the partial truth anyway. He could have been working a case and avoiding Jack at the same time.

"Tell me about your relationship with Nicola," Jack said.

Since Lily was waiting, it was best not to waste any time getting that out there. Plus, he liked that Zeller was off guard. Judging from the way the man's eyes widened and then narrowed, he'd been first surprised by the demand and then riled. Good. Because Jack was riled, too, that a fellow marshal could have withheld something like this.

"There was no relationship," Zeller spat out.

"But you knew her," Jack countered. "And don't bother to deny it, because I have a witness." That last part wasn't exactly true. He had the speculations of a person of interest—Lily—but sometimes a half-truth got fast results. In this case, it did just that.

Zeller groaned and glanced up at the ceiling as if hoping for some kind of divine guidance. "I spoke to Nicola, that's all," he finally admitted. "She'd had a friend who'd gotten involved in the sex trade."

Jack didn't feel one ounce of joy over Zeller's confession, since it was coming way too late. "How'd you find that out?"

Zeller took a deep breath first. "Nicola's name came up when I was questioning a group of college students about the sex-trafficking case. A lot of names came up," he quickly added, "and I talked to a lot of people. Nicola, included."

"Her name wasn't in any of your reports," Jack reminded him.

"No, because I didn't get anything from her. I swear I didn't," Zeller snapped when Jack gave him a hard glare. "My conversation with her lasted less than ten minutes, and I realized her friend didn't have anything to do with my investigation. She was just someone who got lured into turning tricks by her sleazy boyfriend."

Jack mentally went through every word of that, and he was sure that Caroline was doing the same. In the squad room, he saw Kellan finish his call and give Jack a thumbs-up. He hoped that meant his brother had gotten the process started for the warrant for the other computer files at New Beginnings.

Jack turned his attention back to Zeller, who was clearly waiting for him to continue. "So, if your meeting with Nicola was all innocent, as you say, why not mention you'd met her once her body had been discovered?"

"At first I didn't remember talking to her. Not until I saw photos of her body." His breath turned into a long sigh. "And then I started feeling guilty, thinking that maybe something I said spurred her to do something dangerous. Like trying to save other girls like her friend."

Jack latched right onto that. "Was that what Nicola was trying to do?"

"I don't know. That's the truth," Zeller added in a hoarse whisper. "Like I said, I had a short conversation with her, one I barely remember, but I guess it's possible she picked up on something that made her put herself in a situation that turned dangerous."

Yes, it was. But then it was just as likely that Nicola had struck out on her own to try to investigate something she should have left to the badges. Of course, in this case, maybe the *badge* was what had gotten her into trouble if she'd inadvertently mentioned something to Zeller that made him believe she was some kind of threat. Perhaps Nicola had even known something about his involvement in the sex trafficking.

But if so, Jack had no proof of that.

"Look, I feel like dirt over what happened to her," Zeller went on. "She seemed like a good kid, and she was killed. It doesn't matter that I didn't have anything to do with that. She's still dead."

Either Zeller was telling it the way it was, or else he was darn good at putting on an act. If Zeller was feeling guilty, maybe that was the bad vibe Jack was picking up on and it had nothing to do with being dirty.

This time, it was Jack who took a deep breath. "Just cool your heels for a while. I'll need an official statement from you about Nicola, but for now I have to observe another interview."

"Lily," Zeller quickly supplied. "I heard about the warrant to get the file of the missing woman."

Of course, he had. There wasn't much of a chance of keeping a warrant a secret, and Zeller likely had his ear to the ground to hear anything going on with the investigation. Jack couldn't fault him for that. If their positions had been reversed, he would be doing the same thing.

"I want to be in on Lily's interview," Zeller insisted.

"I'm sure you do, but it's not going to happen." Jack considered telling Zeller that he could watch from the observation room, but Caroline would be in there, and Jack didn't want the marshal near her. "I'll ask Kellan to copy you on the report he writes up after he talks to Lily."

Zeller huffed. "We're on the same side here, Jack. I know you don't believe that." He shot Caroline a nasty glance, no doubt to remind her that she was the reason for the mistrust. But Jack had had his doubts about Zeller before Caroline had voiced any.

"You'll get the report if Kellan agrees," Jack emphasized. "That's the best I can do right now."

Obviously, that wasn't enough in Zeller's opinion. He turned on his heels and stormed out. Jack didn't mind the fit of temper. It was better than the alternative of having Zeller linger around and upset Caroline even more. Jack could practically see the jangled nerves all over her face, but he would need to speak to Zeller again. Would need to make it official that Zeller had neglected to mention the conversation he'd had with a woman who had ended up murdered.

When Kellan tipped his head toward the interview room, Jack and Caroline followed him there. Jack intended to leave Caroline in observation while he conducted the interview with Kellan. But before they could even start, Lily came out, with her lawyer trailing right behind her.

"Are you really trying to get a warrant to get into my computer files?" Lily demanded, and she aimed that at Jack. There was fire in her eyes and raw anger in her voice.

"Yes, Kellan and I are," Jack confirmed. He didn't want Lily including Caroline in on the venom.

Lily made a sound of outrage and batted away her lawyer, who tried to whisper something in her ear. "You have no right!" And this time, she directed her anger solely at Jack. "I'm trying to help women who've been violated."

"If that's all you're doing, then having us look at your files shouldn't be a problem." In contrast, Jack kept his voice calm.

Clearly, it was a problem for Lily, because every muscle in her face tightened in rage. "I'll stop you. So help me, I'll stop you."

"Under the circumstances, my client and I need to reschedule this interview," the lawyer said.

Jack considered nixing any rescheduling, but he rethought that. Maybe it would be best to speak to Lily after the warrant had come through and they'd done a computer search. That way, they might have some ammunition they could use to get her to confess to any wrongdoings going on at New Beginnings. Of course, it was possible for Lily to successfully fight the warrant. That had been known to happen, but if she managed it, that would make her look as if she were hiding something.

"Tomorrow morning," Jack finally said. "Be back here at nine."

That should give them plenty of time to press for the warrant and start searching through the files. He had no idea how many women were actually in the facility or had been there, but the search might take a while.

And it was something Caroline could help them with.

He'd likely run into some protest from Kellan on that, but Jack understood that Caroline needed to be part of this. She should have a hand in helping eliminate the threat to both of them. Besides, Caroline would get through those files a lot faster than Kellan, he or the techs they could get to work on it.

Lily certainly didn't thank Jack for rescheduling. As Zeller had done, she hightailed it out of there, leaving the anger still vibrating in the air.

"I'd better push on that warrant," Kellan muttered, taking out his phone again. As he'd done with the other call, he stepped into the squad room.

"I'm okay," Caroline told Jack before he could even ask. "Really," she added when he gave her a flat look. She sighed and pushed her hair from her face. "I just want answers. I want the person who attacked us behind bars."

"That's my top priority," he said, though that was one of those half-truths similar to the one he'd told Zeller.

Finding the person responsible and keeping Caroline safe and sane went hand in hand. But Jack knew that once that happened, it wouldn't be the end of things. Caroline still had to recover from the ordeal that Eric had put her through. She'd need time to deal not only with that but also with her feelings for him. And she did have feelings. No doubts about that. But Jack suspected that was the last thing she wanted to sort out right now.

"Sorry I dragged you in here," Jack told her.

Caroline lifted her shoulder. "You didn't get to do the interview, but we still learned some things. Both Lily and Zeller are scared. Maybe they're that way only because of the damage something like this can do to their reputations, but they're scared."

Oh, yeah. And Jack liked that because it could perhaps cause them to make a mistake. It could also make them dangerous. If one of them had indeed run the sex-trafficking ring and murdered Nicola, then there was nothing they'd hesitate to do to cover their tracks.

Because getting caught could lead to the death penalty.

"If Lily tries to delete or hide computer files, we can arrest her," Jack explained. "Ditto if Zeller tries to cover up the unreported contact he had with Nicola."

Of course, neither of those things would be a direct link to the attack, but it could open a door or two. Right now, Jack would settle for a sliver of an opening.

He was about to suggest that Caroline and he go back to his place to work, but before he could say anything, his phone rang. Jack frowned when Unknown Caller popped up on the screen.

Hell, what now?

He hit the answer button, and while hoping that whatever he was about to hear didn't give them another dose of bad news, he put the call on Speaker. "Marshal Jack Slater," he answered.

Jack didn't care much for the long silence that followed, but he finally heard a woman's voice. "Marshal, you've been trying to get in touch with me. I'm Grace Wainwright. I understand you have some questions for me."

Well, he certainly hadn't expected Kingston's friend, and the former resident of New Beginnings, to return his call. Jack had figured he'd have to track her down.

"Yes, I have questions," he verified. "What

can you tell me about an attack that took place yesterday near Longview Ridge?"

Since it was a direct question, he thought maybe she would dodge it. She didn't. "Unfortunately, I know more about it than I should." Grace sighed, and it sounded both heavy and weary. "Marshal Slater, there are some things you need to know about Caroline Moser."

Chapter Ten

Caroline couldn't stop the new round of fear and worry that slammed through her when she heard what Grace Wainwright had just said.

There are some things you need to know about Caroline Moser.

She didn't think she had blank spots left in her memory, but it was possible she did. Also possible that this woman was about to give her news that she wouldn't want to hear. Wouldn't want Jack to hear, either. Still, that didn't stop Caroline from moving closer to the phone so that she wouldn't miss a word.

"Where are you?" Jack asked Grace.

It was one of those square-filler questions that lawmen needed to ask. A face-to-face interview was better than one on the phone, and there was the troubling problem of Grace's safety. If she was involved in this—whatever *this* was—then she could be in danger.

"Sorry, but I'd rather keep my location to myself," Grace answered. She didn't sound angry or resentful. In fact, her voice was surprisingly calm.

"That might not be smart," Jack countered. "I could help you."

"Thanks, but I'll manage. I don't exactly trust lawmen and cops."

Caroline couldn't muster up a nod of agreement when Jack shot her a glance.

"By now, I suspect you've talked to Kingston and Lily?" Grace went on.

Jack paused, obviously considering how much to tell Grace. And when to press her on what she intended to tell him about Caroline. "I have. What do they have to do with Caroline and you?"

Grace made a sound, a sort of hollow laugh. "Everything. Or at least, I think everything. It's all balled up together, you see."

"No, I don't see. Spell it out for me," Jack insisted. "What did you want to tell me about Caroline?"

"That she's part of this. Not the crimes. Not the murders. But she's a part of it."

"All right," Jack huffed. "Keep talking. And I'm especially interested in hearing if you helped your old buddy Kingston get to Caroline."

Definitely no laugh this time. "I didn't. Is that what he told you, that I helped him?"

"Kingston said plenty," Jack settled for saying.

Grace gave another heavy sigh. "Well, I didn't give Kingston any information about anyone. Especially not Caroline. She's in WITSEC, which would have meant me hacking into federal files."

Jack lifted an eyebrow. "You aren't good enough to tap those files?" And this time he was obviously goading Grace, probably hoping to spur her into blurting out more than she intended.

"I'm good at digging out data," Grace answered. "I'm sure you've already heard that, but I wouldn't have done something to bring the feds, or you, coming after me. Especially you. You would have hounded me to the ends of the earth to get back at me for going after your woman."

Your woman. So Grace knew about their relationship. Something like that wouldn't have been hard to access, but what wouldn't have been so easy was getting to the depths of Jack's feelings, which would have indeed caused him to go after Grace and bring her to justice. It meant Grace had been thorough when she'd gotten whatever she had on Jack and her.

"How did you know I was in WITSEC?" Caroline asked, knowing that it was going to earn her a scowl from Jack.

It did.

He obviously had wanted her to stay quiet, maybe because he thought Grace wouldn't spill all if she knew someone else was listening, but Caroline had taken a calculated risk. There was a reason Grace had dug into their relationship. Into their situation. And she'd called Jack. Apparently, the woman had something to say.

"Everything pointed to you being in WITSEC," Grace explained. "When the cops found you in Longview Ridge, Eric was still alive. No way would Marshal Slater have risked Eric getting to you again, and with your head injury, WITSEC is the only thing that made sense."

Maybe. But it was possible that Grace had confirmed that by hacking into Justice Department files. Of course, that only led Caroline to yet more questions. Why would Grace have done that? Why was the woman so interested in her?

"I've been looking into Nicola Gunderson's murder," Grace went on before Caroline could press her for more. "And no, I didn't know her, but her murder grabbed my attention." She paused. "I felt sorry for her, that she died that way."

Caroline looked at Jack to see if he believed that last part, but he only shrugged. It was possible what Grace was saying was true. Nicola's death had gotten the attention of a lot of people. An attractive college student who'd been kidnapped and forced into sex trafficking, only to be murdered. Of course, the media hadn't picked up on Zeller's connection to Nicola.

But did Grace know?

Since that would be giving the woman too much information on their conversation with Zeller, Caroline kept it to herself and waited for Grace to continue. She didn't have to wait long.

"After Nicola's murder and Eric's death, I started researching the investigation," Grace explained. "I believe whoever was running the sex trafficking got Eric to kill Nicola."

Caroline felt that hot tightness in her stomach. "Why do you think that?" she snapped. This time the memories came with a hefty dose of anger. Mercy, were they going to have to add another name to Eric's list of murders?

"Because of info I got from hacking into some files. And no, I won't tell you specifically which ones, because if you do manage to find me, I don't want to be arrested for it."

Caroline could see the debate going on in Jack's eyes. No way could he offer Grace immunity, because hacking was a serious crime. Plus, the woman might not even be telling the truth.

"Does the name Skylar Greer mean anything to you?" Grace asked.

That got every bit of Caroline's attention. Jack's, too, because his eyes widened, then narrowed. "What about her?" Jack countered, obviously keeping his investigative cards close to the chest.

"She was in the sex-trafficking ring, too, and was rescued," Grace went on after a long pause. "Afterward, Skylar started asking questions and was trying to figure out who'd been running the ring."

Caroline didn't think it was much of a stretch that the woman had done that while living at New Beginnings.

"Do you know where Skylar is?" Jack asked.

"No." Grace didn't hesitate before that answer. "But it's possible she's in hiding. I hope she is, anyway. I hope her questions didn't get her killed."

Caroline hoped the same thing, and it twisted away at her to think of the worst-case scenario here. That Skylar may have been murdered by the same person responsible for taking her into the sex-trafficking ring.

Maybe Lily or Zeller.

Heck, maybe even Kingston. Grace had said

this was all balled up together, and Kingston was definitely in the mix.

"Do you know if Skylar saw a counselor or therapist while she was at New Beginnings?" Jack pressed, and Caroline knew why. If she had, then that should have been in the file.

"I'm not sure. Maybe," Grace concluded. "She was eager to turn her life around. Eager to find answers, too, and I think it was that search for the truth that maybe landed her in trouble."

Jack gave an impatient huff. "What did Skylar find in that search and how is all of this connected to Caroline?"

"Again, I'm not sure what she found." Grace hesitated. "But I believe whatever Skylar learned, someone wanted her silenced for it. And that leads me back to Caroline. If Eric did kill Nicola at the request of the person running the sex-trafficking ring, then that person might believe Eric told Caroline about it. Eric had her a long time, and he was cocky. He could have bragged to her about it."

Yes, Eric was cocky, but he'd never mentioned Nicola. Of course, that didn't mean anything. Eric had only talked about his murders in a general kind of way. He'd been far more interested in taunting Caroline for not figuring out sooner that he was a serial killer. The taunts had been like an arrow to her heart because they'd been true.

"Do you have any proof to back up what you're saying?" Jack asked Grace.

"None. It's based on conversations and files that no longer exist. Someone wiped them. Someone who almost certainly wanted to cover up their crimes. I'll leave that to you to figure out."

"Obviously, you wanted to help with that or you wouldn't have returned my call," Jack quickly pointed out.

"No, I returned your call to get you off my back. Also to warn you that I believe this all goes back to Caroline and what the killer thinks Eric might have told her. I don't want to be dragged out into the open so I can be silenced."

That was another arrow strike. Maybe Skylar and Nicola had both been killed to protect a killer's identity. A fatal tying up of loose ends. Both Grace and she also could fall into that category, but there was one major difference between them. Grace obviously knew a lot more about this than Caroline did.

"I want you to back off and not try to contact me again," Grace added, and before Jack could say anything, she ended the call.

Cursing, Jack immediately hit Redial to call Grace back. No answer, and Caroline was betting the woman had used a burner cell, so there was no way to trace it.

"She hacked into the New Beginnings files," Caroline concluded, and she got an instant nod of agreement from Jack.

"That's why I need to talk to her again and find out if something was deleted from Skylar's record." He looked at her. "Any chance you can find Grace?"

"I'll try. I don't know her, not personally, but it's possible we brushed up against each other in cyberspace."

Jack's eyes narrowed a little, enough to let her know that he didn't want that "brushing up" to get her into legal hot water.

"I'll be careful," Caroline assured him.

He studied her a moment, then went to her and brushed a kiss on her cheek. Considering the heat that was always there between them, it seemed almost chaste. Something she hadn't thought possible from Jack. He eased back, their gazes connecting and holding for a long time. Too long. Because she saw more than the fire fueled by the attraction; she saw the worry he had for her.

"I'll be careful," she repeated, and this time Caroline was the one who dropped a kiss on his cheek.

He studied her a moment longer as if he

wanted to say more, and then he tore his attention from her. "I'll get you a computer."

Jack went into the bullpen and spoke to Gunnar, and a few moments later, the deputy took a laptop from one of the empty desks and handed it to Jack. Jack was on his way back to Kellan's office when Caroline saw the visitor come in.

Kingston.

She was still feeling raw from everything that had already gone on, but she didn't mind going around again with him. Everything she and Jack learned could put them a step closer to catching their attacker, and Caroline was positive that Kingston knew more than he'd told them.

Jack, however, didn't seem as eager to meet with one of their persons of interest, and it was obvious he didn't trust Kingston, because Jack immediately stepped in between Caroline and him. Then Jack passed her the computer, no doubt to free up his hands. Since she wanted to do the same thing, Caroline put the laptop on Kellan's desk.

"I'm here to sign the statement that I gave to your brother," Kingston said. "Somebody called and told me it was ready."

"I did," Gunnar spoke up. "Give me a sec, and I'll get it for you."

Kingston didn't go to the deputy. He stayed put and cast glances at both Jack and her. "I gotta say that the two of you don't make many friends. I was at the diner across the street and saw Lily when she came out. She didn't seem happy."

"She wasn't," Jack verified. In the same breath he added, "What were you doing at the diner?"

"Waiting on a call that the report was ready. There's a storm moving in, and I thought I'd go ahead and drive out here while the weather was still clear." Kingston got that smug look on his face, as if pleased that he'd had a plausible answer.

Gunnar came to the doorway and handed Kingston the report and a pen. "Look that over and let me know if there are any corrections that need to be made."

Kingston nodded and moved as if to step away, but Jack stopped him. "I just had an interesting conversation with someone you know. Grace Wainwright."

Like Jack, Caroline was watching Kingston's face, and she saw it. The flash of concern. "Grace? What did she want? Where is she?"

The last question seemed to only increase his concern. But Caroline didn't know where that particular emotion of his was aimed. Was he worried about an old friend, or did Kingston think Grace had given them info they could use against him?

"She's fine," Jack answered. "Safe."

Caroline figured that last part was wishful thinking on Jack's part, along with being bait to see more of Kingston's reaction.

"Good," Kingston said, but his expression didn't mesh with the response. "I was worried about her. Grace tends to champion causes that can get her into trouble."

Interesting. And Caroline didn't believe it was her imagination that Kingston had thought carefully about how he was going to say that.

"What causes did Grace recently champion?" Jack asked.

Kingston lifted his shoulder. "I don't have anything specific, but that's just the way Grace is."

Jack stared at him. "Nothing specific, huh? Nothing about the woman missing from New Beginnings?"

"Oh, that." Kingston dismissed it with his tone. "Yes, I suppose it's possible Grace would have poked around with that. She would have likely known the woman since they were at New Beginnings together." He lifted the reports. "I'll just find someplace quiet to go over this."

Jack stepped in front of him before he could

leave. "Does Lily have any reason to harm Caroline or want to silence her?" Jack asked.

Kingston huffed and shook his head. "I don't have any details about the sex-trafficking ring. If Lily had a part in that, I don't have proof."

"Any other reason you can think of?" Jack pressed. "Something that's perhaps connected to Eric Lang?"

Again, Kingston shook his head and turned as if to leave, but then he stopped. "Maybe Lily's still upset about the Crime-Track program that Caroline and Gemma were working on."

Of all the things Caroline had thought Kingston might say, that wasn't one of them. "Crime-Track? Why would Lily be upset about that?"

"Lily tried to invest in it," Kingston calmly said.

Jack immediately looked at her as Caroline said, "I don't remember that." And she didn't. She was sure there hadn't been a single conversation about Lily when it came to Crime-Track. Unless she truly had gaps in her memory and this one had slipped through.

"I don't think she advertised her interest in it," Kingston explained, "but she contacted Gemma. Lily wanted to fund the project, but Gemma turned her down. It might have caused some bad blood between them."

Jack took out his phone and handed it to Caroline so she could call Gemma. She went to the other side of Kellan's office while she did that. Not that the distance would give her much privacy, but at least Kingston wouldn't be able to hear her every word.

Caroline scrolled through the contacts, pressed Gemma's number and said a quick prayer of thanks when Gemma answered on the first ring.

"Is everything okay?" Gemma quickly asked. "Was there another attack?"

"No. We're fine," Caroline assured her, and she felt guilty that she'd caused her friend an obvious moment of terror. Not just because of Jack and her but also because the man Gemma loved could have been in the line of fire.

The breath of relief Gemma took was audible. "Sorry. I'm on edge."

Caroline was right there with her. Too bad things would stay that way until they made an arrest. This phone call might help with that.

"I have a question about Crime-Track," Caroline explained. "Did Lily Terrell ever contact you about it?"

"Yes," Gemma answered after a short pause. "She dropped by my office shortly after the project started, before you started working on it."

So that was why Caroline hadn't recalled anything about this. "You didn't want Lily involved with it?"

"No. Because Lily didn't want to merely be involved. She wanted control of the project."

Control? Caroline tried to think of a logical reason for that. Maybe because Lily believed she could use it to help with stopping things like sex trafficking? But that seemed a stretch since the program was being designed to catch killers.

"It was hard to turn down the funding that Lily offered," Gemma added, "but I wanted the data and reports to be as objective as possible. For that to happen, I thought it best if I handled the process. For all the good that did," she muttered.

Maybe Gemma hadn't meant for her to hear that, but she did. And Caroline couldn't even argue with Gemma on that point or try to make her friend feel better. Because Eric had made dupes out of both of them.

"Was Lily angry when you turned down her funding?" Caroline asked.

"Possibly. I mean, she didn't yell or anything, but she also didn't contact me again. Once when I saw her at a party, she didn't even speak to me."

That sounded like anger to Caroline, but she couldn't see it leading to attempted murder. If it had, Lily would have likely gone after Gemma instead of Jack and her.

"You're staying safe, right?" Caroline pressed, just to make sure.

"Of course." Gemma huffed. "Kellan has one of the reserve deputies guarding me, and the ranch hands are on alert."

"Good. Keep it that way."

"What's this all about?" Gemma demanded. "Was Lily involved in the attack?"

"We're not sure. If she is, you'll be one of the first to know. Take care of yourself, Gemma."

When Caroline finished the call and turned back around to hand Jack his phone, she realized Kingston was gone. "I sent him to the interview room so he could read the report," Jack said. "I figured you didn't want him hanging around here."

"I don't." The guy made her extremely uneasy. Of course, any admirer of Eric would. "Did Kingston tell you anything else about Lily?"

Jack shook his head. "Did you get anything from Gemma?"

Caroline put it in a nutshell. "Lily wanted control of the project, and Gemma refused. I'm not sure if it plays into this, though."

He made a sound of agreement. "Hard to see how it would fit. Well, unless Lily thought she could manipulate the program for some kind of vigilante justice or to launch her own illegal spree. Yeah, I know, it's a long shot," he added.

It was, but… "When Crime-Track first started,

it was all about gathering data about murders. The idea was to use that data to try to predict when and where other killings would take place and to combine that with profiles to identify possible suspects. It was meant to become a tool for law enforcement, but maybe someone with unlawful intent would want to stop the project in its tracks."

Jack nodded. "And one way for Lily to do that would be to fund it and then crush it."

Yes, but that seemed like an inefficient way to hide her criminal tracks. Still, it was a possible piece that Jack and she could eventually fit into this puzzle of an investigation.

Before Jack could even put his phone away, it rang, and she saw the muscle flicker in his jaw when he looked at the screen.

"It's Teagan," Jack said, and for a moment Caroline thought he was going to put the call on speaker so she could hear any updates on the case. He didn't. And he stepped away from her when he answered.

Combined with the tight jaw and his sudden secretiveness, this couldn't be good. Nor was the fact that he was practically whispering his fast-clipped responses. She heard him say "What?" Then he followed it with some profanity.

The conversation didn't last long. Less than a

minute. But Caroline was certain that Jack had just gotten bad news.

"What's wrong?" she demanded the moment he finished the call.

He took his time answering, which only put her more on edge. "Teagan did a scan of the laptop you used at the WITSEC house, and she found a new tracker called Geo-Trace on one of the sites you accessed. A site about Eric Lang."

She listened carefully to each word, processing it and Jack's dark mood that went along with the explanation. "Geo-Trace," she repeated. "It was still in the experimental stage last I checked."

Jack nodded. "It's apparently operational now, and someone put it on that site."

It didn't take her long to fill in the blanks. "And that someone used my search to track me to the location of the house."

He met her eye to eye. "Yes."

Caroline groaned and pressed her fists against each side of her head. "How could I have been so stupid?"

"You didn't know," he simply said, and it was layered with sympathy. Something she didn't want. Didn't deserve. What she'd done was more than just stupid, though. It had nearly gotten them killed. "God, Jack. I'm so sorry."

"Don't," he warned her, and he went to her,

pulling her into his arms. "This isn't your fault. It's the fault of the person who put the tracker on the site."

There was something else in his voice now. Anger. And she didn't think it was directed at her—even though it should have been.

Think, she demanded, fighting her way through the emotions that were flooding her mind. *Think*. Had the Geo-Trace been put on the site specifically to find her?

Possibly.

If so, she didn't have to guess why that'd happened. The person wanted her dead, and it almost certainly went back to the night Eric had taken her hostage. Either someone thought Eric had told her something or that she'd overheard or seen it. Something that her attacker wanted to keep hidden, and the way to do that was to silence her permanently. Jack would just be collateral damage.

"There's more," Jack went on. "I asked the computer guys to do a reverse search to try to find out who put Geo-Trace on the site. And they found the source."

The relief came, but it didn't last. That was because Caroline knew that this wasn't good news.

"Zeller," he said, his voice clipped. "Geo-Trace was loaded on the site from Zeller's office computer."

Chapter Eleven

While Jack slogged his way through the list of calls he had to make, he kept his eye on Caroline. She was at a small table that he'd moved into Kellan's office specifically for her, working on the borrowed laptop. Trying to track down Grace.

He also suspected she was trying to deal with her feelings.

Even though she wasn't talking about it, Caroline was probably still burdened with guilt over the whole Geo-Trace problem. And yeah, she was blaming herself. Jack certainly wasn't. He was putting the blame right where it belonged.

On Zeller.

Well, if Zeller was actually responsible, that is. Jack was trying to sort through his own feelings and questions about that.

It would have been incredibly stupid for a marshal to use his computer to install a tracking device like that. Something that could be traced right back to him. So, unless Zeller had gotten careless, it meant someone had perhaps set him up. And that was a question Jack intended to ask Zeller as soon as he arrived.

Jack checked his watch. One o'clock already. Which meant Zeller should get to the sheriff's office anytime now. Jack hadn't given the man a heads-up on what the visit was about, but it was possible that Zeller had gotten word about what had been found on his computer. It was hard to keep something like that quiet when others in the office would have known that the techs were running checks.

Still, it didn't matter if Zeller knew or if he'd had time to come up with a story to cover his tracks. A face-to-face meeting would allow Jack to look into his eyes and maybe see if he was telling the truth.

Jack gave Caroline another glance before he went into the squad room to refill his coffee. Kellan was there, doing the same, and he'd no doubt take that fresh cup to the interview room where he'd been working for the past couple hours. His choice, not Jack's. Jack had offered to move Caroline and himself into that room, but Kellan had insisted they stay in his office.

"How's she doing?" Kellan asked, tipping his head to Caroline.

She didn't look up at them. She kept her attention nailed to the laptop screen while her fingers seemingly flew over the keyboard. Next to it was the untouched sandwich that Jack had had delivered for her from the diner. Soon, he'd try to coax her again into eating.

Jack didn't sugarcoat the truth when he answered Kellan. "She's not doing that well. Way too much has happened in the past twenty-four hours, and it's a lot to take on."

Kellan gave a grunt of agreement and sipped his coffee. "Does 'way too much' include you two sleeping together?"

Jack nearly snapped that it was none of Kellan's business, but he knew his brother hadn't meant to pry into his personal life. The bottom line was that sex had complicated things. It had made Jack less objective—though he couldn't remember a time when objectivity had played into his feelings for Caroline.

"It does include that," Jack admitted. He rubbed his forehead, where a dull ache throbbed. "I love her and I want to protect her. If you can figure out a way to stay objective about that, I'd like to hear it."

Maybe because Kellan knew that Jack was dealing with as much emotion as Caroline, he wisely held back any judgment or advice. Kellan just patted his brother on the back and headed toward the interview room. Jack went the other direction. He got Caroline a cup of coffee and brought it to her in the office.

"Thanks," she muttered, not looking up at him, but then she stopped, her fingers still poised over the keyboard.

"Problem?" he asked, knowing there were plenty of them. He just hoped there wasn't something new, since they were already grappling with enough.

"There's no sign of Grace. And the phone she used was indeed a burner." Caroline paused long enough to gulp down some coffee. "I put out feelers through old contacts. *Safe* feelers," she emphasized. "I don't want the wrong person finding her, so I only emailed people I trust."

Good. Because they didn't know who the wrong person was—yet. But it was possible that Grace could become a target if she surfaced.

"I also ran a deeper background check on her," Caroline went on. "Unlike some of the other women who were kidnapped and drugged into the sex-trafficking ring, Grace was lured into it through her drug habit. From everything I'm hearing, she's clean now, but when she was using, she was out of it. Out of it enough to turn tricks to support her habit."

Jack thought about that a moment. "Any idea who got Grace to start turning tricks?"

She shook her head. "Nothing so far, but I

think it's important to find that out. Maybe it was one of our suspects, and if so, we could use Grace to tie Zeller, Lily or Kingston to the rest of what's happening."

He was thinking the same thing. But first, they had to find Grace and convince the woman to trust them. Then he'd have to persuade her to tell all and go into protective custody. No easy feat to do that when it was obvious the woman didn't even want to be found.

Jack slid the plate with the sandwich closer to Caroline's hand, and she glanced at it as if seeing it for the first time. Which was probably true. Caroline tended to get wrapped up when she was doing research.

She frowned but took a bite of the ham-and-Swiss that he knew was her favorite. "There's more," Caroline said, chasing the sandwich with coffee. "I did some checking on Geo-Trace—"

He groaned. "Not a good idea. The Justice Department is all over that. Please tell me you didn't hack into their files."

"I didn't." She was quick to assure him of that. "I went through my own sources, and what I got isn't proof. More of the opinion of others like me."

In other words, hackers. Probably many of them with criminal records. Jack didn't groan again, but that was what he wanted to do.

"Geo-Trace could be a fake," Caroline added after she gave him a couple of seconds to rein in his temper.

Jack went still, letting that sink in. Or rather, trying to let that happen. But he had to shake his head. "But Teagan had heard of it, and it was on the computer."

"There's plenty of talk about it," she verified, "but I'm just not finding the proof that someone has perfected it enough to make it do what it's being designed to do—cull out that kind of info from an IP address."

Jack wasn't a computer idiot, but he also knew this was a conversation that could quickly go over his head. "Put that in layman's terms for me."

She nodded, paused again, this time with her forehead bunching up. "Other than the Geo-Trace that you found on my laptop and Zeller's computer, it doesn't show up anywhere else. That's an electronic red flag because you can bet that someone would have used this program if it were actually available."

Yeah, Jack could see that. Stalkers, thieves and other assorted scum would want their hands on it so they could track the physical location of someone simply because they were using a computer with an internet connection.

"I think the Geo-Trace was just a ruse," Caroline went on. "Something designed to make us think my location had been compromised through the laptop."

If so, that meant someone had set Zeller up.

"Yes," Caroline said as if she'd known exactly what he was thinking.

Since Zeller could arrive any minute, Jack shut the office door so that Caroline and he could have the rest of this conversation without the possibility of Zeller coming in on it.

"It doesn't mean Zeller is innocent, though," she continued. "Maybe I'm wrong about Geo-Trace. It could be that he got his hands on a working program. And even if he didn't, he might be going for some kind of reverse psychology. He might want to make himself look innocent by making us believe someone set him up."

That was something he'd need to give more thought, but Jack could see it from that angle. "Perhaps Zeller or someone else put this fake tracer on your computer and his so it would conceal the fact that the WITSEC file on you had actually been hacked. Geo-Trace would be a way of covering up the hacking."

She stayed quiet a moment, obviously giving that some thought. "It's possible. But it would have taken some serious skills to set all of this in motion."

Jack agreed, and that led him to the next question. "Who's capable of doing something like this?" And one name instantly came to mind. "Grace?"

"Maybe. I don't know how good she is. But I've been in touch with some of my old contacts, and one name keeps coming up. Scotty Milford."

Now, that was a familiar name. "If it's the same guy I'm thinking about, he's a criminal informant."

She nodded. "It's the same guy. He got busted a few years ago for cybercrimes, and he's clean-ish."

"Clean-ish?" Jack scowled. Cursed. "Is that like being a little bit pregnant?"

The color actually rose in Caroline's cheeks. Maybe because she was remembering that he hadn't used a condom the night before. He was still kicking himself over that, but the kicks would have to wait. He made a circling motion with his finger for her to continue.

"My contacts are split as to whether or not Scotty is up to his old tricks again," she explained. "He hasn't gotten caught for anything, but he also hasn't been as chatty online as he normally is. Sometimes, being quiet is a way of not letting others know what you're doing."

That was true in the world of law enforcement, too. "You think he could be involved?" he came out and asked.

"Yes," she said without hesitation.

And that was plenty enough for him. Jack took out his phone so he could get Scotty's contact info.

Caroline stood, picking up the notepad she'd been using. "I already have his number. I got it from one of those contacts, but I should be the one to do this. Scotty would be more likely to talk to me about this than a badge."

He didn't have to think long and hard about that. She was right. So he handed her his phone.

"Any chance that your name and number are in Scotty's contacts?" she asked. "Because I don't want 'Marshal Jack Slater' flashing on the screen."

"I haven't talked to him in a while, and I've gotten a new number since then."

With a nod, she pressed in the number from her notepad, put the call on speaker and waited. After three rings, the call went to voice mail. He saw the brief debate she had with herself about what to do, but she left a message.

"Scotty, this is Caroline Moser," she said. "Call me back at this number ASAP. It's important."

Good. Of course, if Scotty did call, Jack would have to pass his phone to Caroline. He didn't want the man hanging up on them before he even got the chance to question him.

Jack saved the number Caroline had dialed to call the man and put it under Scotty's name. He was still in the process of putting his phone away when there was a knock at the door. As he'd done since this whole ordeal with Caroline started, he moved in front of her and made sure it would be easy for him to reach his weapon before he answered it. The person standing there was exactly who Jack had expected it to be.

Zeller.

And surprise, surprise, he wasn't happy.

Jack had riled Zeller so much in the past twenty-four hours that he was going to owe him a huge apology if it turned out that the marshal was innocent. But Jack had no intentions of believing in that innocence just yet.

There was water dripping off Zeller's hair and running down his face, and that caused Jack to glance out the front windows. The storm had moved in all right, and it was pouring.

"I didn't put anything on Caroline's computer that caused the location of her house to be breached," Zeller spat out, though Jack wasn't sure how he could even talk with his jaw muscles that tight.

"Who told you about that?" Jack immediately asked.

Jack hadn't thought it possible, but the muscles tightened even more. "I have friends at the office, and one of them alerted me that you went behind my back and had my computer checked."

"I did," Jack readily admitted. "And as you obviously know, the techs found something. Care to explain how that tracking program got from your laptop to Caroline's?"

Of course, if Caroline's theory was right, a hacker could have made it look as if Zeller's computer had been used. But no way was Jack going to share that with a man who might want them dead.

Zeller opened his mouth as if ready to shout out an argument, but then he stopped and lowered his shaking head. He stayed that way for several long moments before his attention came back to Jack.

"I didn't do this," Zeller said, his voice weary and hoarse now. "I'm being set up, and the person's doing a damn good job of it. I'm being investigated and people are talking. Even when I'm cleared of the computer charges——and I will be—my reputation will be hurt."

In the beginning, it would be. Jack couldn't see a way around that, but a bruised reputation was a small price to pay for getting away with murder. Heck, Zeller could get away with the computer charges, too, because there might not be enough evidence to pin this on him. A lawyer could argue that plenty of other marshals would have had access to his workplace computer.

"It's either Kingston or Lily who's doing this," Zeller went on. "Kingston maybe because he's carrying out some sick beyond-the-grave orders from Eric." He looked at Caroline. "You know that Eric was capable of doing something like that."

She nodded. "Eric was capable of a lot of things, but he liked to taunt. That's not happening here. The tracer on the site was, well, sneaky. And, yes, Eric could have managed to get someone to do that, but he would have wanted me to know that he'd bested me even after he was dead."

Caroline was right, but Jack could mentally play devil's advocate and see this from a different side. Kingston could have done it as an homage to a twisted SOB that he admired. If so, Kingston might not be in the mindset of gloating and taunting.

And that left Lily.

Jack wasn't sure if Lily had the computer skills, but the woman had enough money to hire someone. Plus, setting up Zeller and having him arrested and convicted would definitely get any heat off her.

"You were getting a warrant on the files at

New Beginnings," Zeller continued a moment later. "Lily's stonewalling that, and it could be because she's got plenty to hide."

Jack could feel himself scowling. "How did you know about the warrant request?" he asked Zeller.

But Jack immediately waved that off. If Zeller had heard about the computer tracker being linked back to them, then he could have easily heard about the warrant. In fact, he would have taken that as some possible light at the end of a very dark tunnel if they could use that warrant to find anything to incriminate Lily.

Since Zeller had brought it up, Jack took out his phone and texted Teagan to get an update on the warrant. His partner answered right away.

Lily's lawyers are trying to block the warrant, Teagan messaged. They're claiming some of the files have medical info protected under the law. It might take a while to get it all sorted out.

Hell. They didn't have a while. A delay like this could give Lily a chance to destroy any evidence that might be in those files. Jack consoled himself, though, with the thought that a smart person would have already made sure there was nothing incriminating to find.

"Just let the investigation of your computer play out," Jack told Zeller. "If someone planted the tracer to frame you, that will come to light."

He hoped. While Jack still considered Zeller a suspect, he wanted to get to the truth of what was going on.

Zeller's gaze slashed between Caroline and Jack for several moments before the man cursed and walked away. He didn't storm out this time, and there was a weariness to his posture as he exited the building. Of course, Jack was cynical enough to think that anything Zeller did right now could be fake. Part of the facade to make them believe he was innocent.

Caroline stepped to Jack's side and watched until Zeller was out of sight. "Do you think his computer skills are good enough to pull off planting a tracker on multiple websites?"

Jack had to shake his head. "I'm not sure."

But it was something he could find out. If he could have gone into his office, he would have been able to talk to his fellow marshals, but no way was he going to leave Caroline. Or take her into what she'd consider a lion's den, since she didn't have a whole lot of trust for lawmen. That meant he'd just have to rely on getting that info from Teagan.

On a heavy sigh, Caroline moved back to the table where she'd been working, but she stopped when Jack's phone rang again. Scotty's name was on the screen. Jack hadn't expected the hacker to actually return Caroline's call, but he was glad Scotty had. He handed his phone to Caroline again so she could answer.

"Scotty," she said after she put the call on speaker, but that was all she managed to get out before the man interrupted her.

"I'm in trouble, Caroline." Scotty's words were rushed together, and he sounded scared out of his mind. "You've got to help me. God, Caroline, I think someone's trying to kill me."

Chapter Twelve

Caroline felt the punch of dread go through her. No. Not another attack.

"Where are you?" she managed to ask Scotty. "What's wrong?"

"Someone broke into my house," he blurted out. "I ran out back, but I don't like the timing because the break-in came shortly after you left me that message. Did you set someone on me?"

"No. Of course not." And Caroline hated that he felt she would have done something like that. "Where are you?" she repeated. "Who broke into your house?"

"I don't know who it was. Some guy dressed all in black and wearing a ski mask. I was in my home office when I saw the person on my security cam. Then I spotted the gun he was carrying, and I got out, jumped in my car and drove off. But I think the person is following me."

Definitely not good, and it caused Caroline's heart to pound even harder. Mercy, was it possible that someone had indeed used her to get to Scotty? She'd checked for trackers on the websites she'd used, but it was possible one of her contacts had said the wrong thing to the wrong person.

"Scotty?" Jack said. "I'm Marshal Jack Slater. I need you to tell me where you are so I can call someone to help you." He paused, maybe to give Scotty time to react to that, but the only thing Caroline could hear was Scotty mumbling. Or maybe he was praying.

"No cops," Scotty insisted. That came through loud and clear.

Caroline wasn't surprised by that. A lot of hackers, even those who were clean, didn't like the law. Plus, she had her own distrust of cops right now. Not just because of Eric's conversation but also because of Zeller possibly being linked to the attack.

Maybe even linked to this.

Sweet heaven. Was it possible that Zeller had used Scotty to plant that tracker on those sites and had now sent someone to eliminate him? Zeller couldn't be doing it himself because there wouldn't have been nearly enough time for him to get to Scotty in San Antonio.

"It's all over the news that someone tried to kill you, that it happened in Longview Ridge," Scotty went on. "Is that where you are now?"

Caroline certainly didn't jump to answer that. Neither did Jack. And there was a reason for that. It was possible that Scotty wasn't alone, that their would-be killer was in the vehicle with him. Then again, Zeller, Kingston and Lily all knew where she was, so it didn't make the risk any greater to reveal her location to Scotty.

"I'm at the sheriff's office here in Longview Ridge," she finally told him.

"Good, because I'm on my way there now."

Jack didn't curse, but that was what he looked like he wanted to do. "Describe the person and the vehicle that's following you so I can get someone out to help you."

Silence from Scotty, for a long time. "No. Don't send anyone. I don't want to be gunned down or anything. But tell me what's going on. Why is this happening? And I want to hear the answers from Caroline, not you."

Caroline tried to tamp down the whirlwind of thoughts in her head so she could figure out the right thing to say to him. She also tried to steady her breath and her pulse. This wasn't the time for a panic attack.

"I think someone hacked into either WIT-SEC files or a Justice Department computer," she explained. "Did you do that?"

More silence, and like Jack, Scotty cursed this time, too. "You know I'm not going to admit to that. I could go to jail." But then Scotty paused. "Is that why someone's after me?"

It wasn't exactly a confession, but it was close enough. "Who hired you to do that?" Caroline pressed.

But that only caused Scotty to curse even more. "I need your help, not your questions. You need to get out here now and meet me."

"That's not going to happen," Jack spoke up. "Where are you?"

Caroline could tell from Jack's rough tone that he wanted that location so he could call in some of his fellow lawmen, but Scotty didn't answer. Not his question, anyway.

"No!" Scotty yelled.

And Caroline heard something else. The squeal of brakes. The sound of a collision. She also heard Scotty groan, and there was no mistaking that he was in pain.

"Scotty?" Caroline practically shouted.

She repeated his name over and over again, begging him to respond, but she only got more of those moans. The seconds dragged by. Seconds where Scotty could be dying.

"How bad are you hurt?" she pressed. "Tell me where you are, and I can get you some help."

Still, no answer, and she couldn't even hear the moans now. Caroline was about to ask Gunnar to try to trace the call, but he spoke before she could say anything.

"We just got a 911 call about a car accident on the east road, just outside town limits," Gunnar said. "A car hit a light pole."

All of her muscles tightened and twisted. Including the ones in her chest. Caroline had to fight just to drag in a breath. Oh, God. Something bad had happened.

"I'm dispatching an ambulance," Gunnar added, "and I'm on the way there."

Gunnar was already heading for the door when Jack went after him. "It's possible there was an armed suspect in pursuit of the driver. It could be dangerous."

Too dangerous to get an ambulance in there, but the cops would clearly have to respond.

"Help me," Scotty finally groaned out. "I'm dying. Help me."

Caroline figured Jack would give her grief over what she was about to demand, but she was going to do it anyway.

"If Scotty's really dying," she whispered, "I need to try to talk to him. He won't talk to you," she added when Jack opened his mouth. "But he might tell me what he did and who hired him to do it."

Oh, Jack definitely didn't like that, but he couldn't argue her point. This might be their best chance at finding out who had tried to kill them. Of course, there was also a good chance they could be put in another dangerous situation.

"I need you to go with us," Jack told Kellan when he came into the bullpen. "I'll explain along the way."

Kellan didn't hesitate. He hurried toward the door, and the four of them raced out to get into the cruiser. The rain had slowed to just a drizzle, but Jack figured it was only a lull. The storm air felt heavy and the clouds looked ready to burst.

Gunnar took the wheel with Kellan in the front seat, and Jack and she got in the back. While Jack filled Kellan in, Caroline kept her attention on Scotty.

"Are you still there?" she asked Scotty. She kept a tight grip on the phone. "How badly are you hurt?"

"Bad," Scotty managed to say through another of those hoarse groans.

"The ambulance will be right behind us," Kellan let her know, and she relayed that info to Scotty. Whether he understood that or not was anyone's guess.

"Scotty, I need you to tell me who hired you to get into the files," Caroline insisted. "It's important."

Nothing. Not even a groan. And the call disconnected, causing Caroline's concern to sky-rocket. Because someone could be there with Scotty. Someone who wanted to finish what they'd started.

"Who called in the 911?" she asked Gunnar. She tried Scotty's number again, but he didn't answer. Caroline kept trying and silently cursed her now trembling hands.

"Hank Perez," Gunnar answered. "He said he heard a noise, looked at his window and saw that a little red car had slammed into a utility pole. His house is on the hill just above the road, and there are some trees obstructing the view, but he said he could see the front end of the car bashed in and steam pouring from it."

So Hank hadn't actually witnessed the wreck. "Was there another vehicle, someone following the red car?" Caroline pressed.

"Hank didn't say, but he doesn't have the best eyesight. He's in his mideighties."

Yes, Caroline remembered. During the months before Eric had taken her hostage, she'd seen Hank in town a couple of times. "He uses one of those scooters to get around?"

Gunnar verified that with a nod. Part of her was relieved by that because maybe it meant Hank wouldn't go from his house to the car. She didn't want him getting shot by the person who'd been after Scotty. Of course, that person would be a fool to hang around since he or she would have figured someone would call the cops.

It didn't take them long to get down Main Street and onto the rural road that would lead them to Scotty. Hopefully, before it was too late.

Caroline continued pressing in Scotty's number while she kept watch, and despite the drizzle, she still had no trouble seeing the blue SUV that was coming up the road toward them. Maybe the vehicle that had been chasing Scotty. Gunnar must have thought so, too, because he slowed down a little, and both Jack and Kellan drew their weapons.

When the cruiser passed the SUV, Caroline got a glimpse of the driver inside, and her stomach went to her knees.

"That's Grace Wainwright," Caroline told them at the same moment that Jack's phone rang and Grace's name appeared on the screen.

"Should I go after her?" Gunnar asked.

"No," Jack said, "but call for someone else to do that. I want to question her and find out why she was out here." He answered the call as soon as he'd finished those instructions to Gunnar.

"I didn't do anything to hurt Scotty," Grace volunteered the moment she was on the line. "I was trying to help him, but someone ran him off the road."

"Who?" Jack snapped.

"I don't know." Grace made a sobbing sound. "Is Scotty dead?"

"You tell me," Jack countered.

That only caused the woman to cry even louder. "I didn't see the person who did this to him. But I did see Scotty's car. I drove past because I thought someone was in there with him. Someone trying to kill him. I drove away and called 911."

"There was a second call," Kellan verified in a whisper. He was on the phone with someone, probably dispatch.

"I couldn't help Scotty," Grace went on. "I'm so sorry, but I couldn't help him."

The woman sounded genuine, but Caroline had a ton of questions for her. She was certain Jack did, too, but she didn't get any more info from her because Grace ended the call. Maybe the deputy that Gunnar sent out would be able to intercept her and take her to the sheriff's office. Caroline put that thought on hold, though, when she looked ahead and spotted the red car.

Her breath vanished.

Because the car was practically wrapped around the utility pole. She couldn't imagine Scotty or anyone else surviving that kind of collision.

Gunnar pulled the cruiser to a stop, and he threw open his door. Kellan and Jack did the same.

"Stay here," Jack told her. "Let me check things out before you see him."

He was trying to protect her, to shield her from seeing Scotty. Part of her appreciated that, but if there was any chance Scotty was alive, there might not be much time to talk to him.

But she didn't get a chance to remind Jack of that because of the movement in the ditch.

Caroline caught it from the corner of her eye. Just a glimpse of someone next to the old ranch trail that was across the road from Scotty.

And that someone fired a shot at them.

JACK HAD BEEN so focused on getting to Scotty's car that he hadn't seen the shooter in time.

That was a big mistake.

Because the shot slammed into the back window. Right where Caroline was sitting. There was a bullet-resistant panel over the glass, and it held. The window didn't shatter, but Jack also knew it might not hold up if someone continued to fire straight into it. And that was exactly what happened.

A barrage of bullets came, all blasting into that one area of the window. Jack didn't have time to return fire or even pinpoint the shooter. He scrambled back into the cruiser, catching on to Caroline and pulling her down on the seat. She was already about to hunker down, and she tried to drag him with her.

He couldn't take cover, though, and he didn't close his door. Not with his brother and Gunnar out there. So Jack shifted his position and tried to make sure they were okay. Both Gunnar and Kellan were on the road and were crawling their way back to the cruiser.

Gunnar had also left the door open, and like Jack's, it was on the opposite side from the shooter. It would give Kellan and Gunnar two ways to get back into the vehicle.

Well, maybe.

Jack had to rethink that idea when several of the bullets skittered across the surface of the road. None of the shots hit them, but the gunfire did pin them down. Which was likely what the shooter intended to do, because almost immediately, more bullets blasted into the window before the attacker's aim returned to the area near Kellan and Gunnar. Whoever was pulling the trigger definitely had a target in mind.

And that target was Caroline.

He didn't intend to let this snake shoot her, and that meant he had to do something now to stop it. Jack pushed her down on the floorboard so he could move to the side of the cruiser where so many of those shots were being aimed. Not that he was especially eager to get closer to the bullets, but he needed to get a visual on the shooter. And he got one, all right.

"He's in the ditch," Jack muttered under his breath.

The ditch, he knew, was deep and extended for miles. Worse, there were ranch trails where someone could have—and likely had—hidden a vehicle.

In this case, the trail was littered with trees and thick underbrush. Plenty of places for a gunman to use for escape. Jack didn't want to let things get that far, though. He needed this person, preferably alive, so he could get answers.

Their attacker was low enough, the high banks of the ditch acting as cover, and only the person's head, shoulders and weapon were visible. He was wearing a ski mask. Jack couldn't even be sure the shooter was a male, but whoever it was had to have some backup weapons because he or she wasn't taking time to reload. There were only a few seconds in between each new round of gunfire.

"Scotty," Jack heard Gunnar say, and there was plenty of concern in the deputy's voice.

Jack soon saw why. Scotty's car door creaked open, and the man tumbled out onto the ground. He was alive, thank God. That was the good news. But even from the twenty or so feet of distance between them, Jack could see the blood on his shirt. Scotty was clutching his chest.

"He needs an ambulance," Caroline blurted out, and that was when Jack realized she'd lifted her head up enough to look out his open door and toward Scotty.

Yeah, he did need an ambulance, badly, but unfortunately, that wasn't going to happen as long as there was active gunfire in the area. The EMTs would likely have been able to hear the shots over the police radio, but Kellan had also texted someone, too. He'd requested both backup from the sheriff's office and the ambulance.

The EMTs could stay back until they got the all clear, but whoever was coming for backup would move in to help. Maybe that would happen before the bullets ripped the cruiser apart.

"There's nothing we can do for Scotty right now," Jack told her.

He pushed Caroline right back down on the floor, but he couldn't help but notice her face. There wasn't a drop of color in it, and her breathing was way too fast. Heaven knew what kind of flashbacks this was triggering for her, and it might be too much for her to handle.

She frantically shook her head. "Whoever's doing this wants me. If we make him think I'll come out there, he might leave cover enough for Kellan, Gunnar or you to get off a shot."

So Caroline wasn't near the panic stage after all. That didn't mean she was thinking straight, though. "I'm not going to let you go out there," Jack warned her.

"I agree. I think this person would just gun me down. Maybe he'd do the same to you, too." Her words rushed out with her frantic breaths. "But we have to do something. Maybe I can call out to him to distract him, to make him think I'm coming out? We can't just sit here."

Jack was thinking that sitting there was their safest option. They could wait for backup. Or at least that was what he believed until the direction of the shots changed again. There was a new target for the gunman.

Scotty.

Hell. Jack saw the bullets kick up the dirt around where Scotty had fallen. He couldn't tell if any of the shots had actually hit the man, but it was possible that would happen.

Kellan and Gunnar used the shift in gunfire to barrel into the cruiser. First, his brother. Then, Gunnar, who immediately started the engine. He pulled the cruiser up, blocking Scotty from the gunman's shots.

Good. That was a start. It protected an injured man who didn't appear to be armed. But, of course, the gunman just started firing at the cruiser again. They couldn't just drive away, either, and leave Scotty unprotected.

The bullets continued to blast into the rear window over Caroline's head, but even over the deafening sound, Jack heard something else. A siren. Another cruiser was coming up the road toward them.

And just like that, the gunfire stopped.

Part of Jack was glad that someone was no longer trying to kill Caroline, but he knew what the silence meant. The guy was getting away.

"Do you see him?" Jack asked Gunnar and Kellan. He was hoping they had a better vantage point from the front scene, but both shook their heads.

"The shooter's probably using the ditch to put some distance between him and us," Kellan concluded.

Yeah, Jack figured the same thing. "I'm going out there," he said.

That got a loud, quick "No!" from Caroline.

"The gunman could be moving so he can get a shot at Scotty," Jack reminded her.

That didn't exactly stop the protest he saw in her eyes, but she didn't say "No" this time. Instead, she whispered, "Be careful."

He would, but Jack didn't take the time to re-assure her. That was because he needed to get aim on the gunman before he resurfaced and shot Scotty.

Jack got out of the cruiser, and this time he shut his door in case their attacker came out of the ditch with guns blazing. It would be a suicide mission, with three armed lawmen right there and a backup cruiser just seconds away. Still, desperation made people do stupid things.

Hoping to minimize what anyone could label as stupid, Jack used the cruiser for cover, running to the front end of it and keeping down. Keeping watch, too. And it didn't take him long to see what he'd been expecting.

The ski-masked shooter.

The gunman peered out from the ditch, and he'd moved all right. The guy was now a good fifteen yards from the cruiser. He pivoted, taking aim at Scotty. Just as Jack took aim at him.

Jack fired first.

Not just one shot but two, and as much as he wanted answers, he went for the kill instead.

And he got it.

The shots Jack fired took the guy down, and even though he was certain he hadn't missed, he hurried to the ditch to make sure. Keeping his gun aimed and ready, he pulled up next to the ditch and saw the man sprawled in the mud and water that'd been left by the rain.

The guy was dead. Jack was sure of it. But there was someone who was hopefully still alive.

"Get the ambulance in here now!" Jack shouted to Kellan and Gunnar. He started running toward Scotty, and he prayed he wasn't too late to save him.

Chapter Thirteen

Dead.

That was the one word that kept repeating in her head, and Caroline didn't think it would go away anytime soon. Nor would the images of seeing Scotty's car smashed into that utility pole.

She hadn't actually seen his body. Jack was responsible for that. He'd insisted on her staying in the cruiser while the backup and ambulance arrived. Caroline hadn't fought him on that since she'd known in her heart that Scotty was already dead.

So was the gunman.

That didn't ease her frayed nerves, though. She would still hear the sound of all those gunshots and remember the terror she'd felt when Jack stepped outside the cruiser. Yes, she would definitely recall all of that with every detail. And more. She'd have to deal with the worry that this didn't put an end to the danger.

Even though they didn't have an ID yet on the gunman, Caroline figured he'd been hired to kill her. Whoever had done the hiring had likely covered their tracks. Maybe there'd been mistakes made and some evidence or a money trail left behind, but the odds were this would go down as another attempt to get to her.

Caroline drew in slow, deep breaths as Raylene's sister, Deputy Clarie McNeal, pulled the cruiser to a stop in front of Jack's house. Jack had spent most of the drive from the sheriff's office on the phone and keeping watch, but now that they'd arrived at their destination, his focus would be on her.

Or at least it would be once they were inside.

Caroline needed the long breaths not only to try to calm herself but also to try to level out the effects of the adrenaline. If she didn't, Jack would see the panic that was just beneath the surface, and it would make him worry even more than he already did. And there was no mistake about it—he was worried.

It was Clarie who got out first, and ducking against the rain that was coming down hard, she ran to the door, unlocked it and did the security check to make sure no one had gotten inside. Then she motioned for Jack and Caroline, and they hurried in.

"No ID on the gunman yet," Jack told Caroline as he locked the door and reset the alarm. "But we should know something soon. And there is some good news. Lily's turning over the files from New Beginnings."

Wiping the rain from her face, Caroline nodded. That was potentially good. Or at least it would be if Lily hadn't managed to erase any useful information.

Going with that whole attempt to make him not worry, Caroline steeled herself and didn't dodge his gaze when he looked at her. A wary gaze that was examining her for any signs of emotional trauma.

"I'm okay," she assured him.

Judging from the burst of sound that he made, no way was he buying that. Apparently, she wasn't as good at steeling herself as she'd hoped.

"All right," Caroline amended, "maybe I'm not okay exactly, but we're alive and unharmed. That's better than the alternative. Better than Scotty got." It would have been more effective if her voice hadn't cracked on Scotty's name.

Jack glanced at Clarie, who was in the kitchen, and he took Caroline by the arm, leading her to his bedroom. He shut the door, turned to her and started whatever he was about to say.

"You can't blame yourself for any of this," he insisted. He crammed his hands into his pockets, and he probably didn't know that he had blood on his jeans. Not his blood, but Scotty's.

"My guess is that Scotty hacked into WIT-SEC files," Jack went on, "and the person who hired him to do that sent a killer after him today. We got caught up in it."

She couldn't disagree with any part of that; she had already come to the same conclusion. Scotty hadn't deserved to die, but he'd obviously gotten involved with a very dangerous person. Caroline didn't doubt the danger, either, because that same person was likely after her.

"When the cops go through Scotty's files and his home office, they might find something," Jack added. He was clearly trying to soothe her, but she was beginning to think that he needed just as much of that TLC as she did.

Caroline went closer to him. She didn't touch him, though. Not with the powder keg of emotions already in place. Touching him, even for comfort, would fire up heat of a different kind.

"When I left the sheriff's office to go find Scotty, I knew the risk," she said. "But I thought that if we could get answers, it'd be worth it. It would have been," Caroline amended, and she cursed when her voice cracked again.

Jack cursed, too, because despite her facade, she was right on the edge. He did reach for her, and he likely would have triggered that heat by pulling her into his arms. However, he didn't get a chance to do that because his phone rang.

"Grace," Jack grumbled when he looked at the screen.

Caroline definitely hadn't expected a call from the woman, but maybe this was a good sign. Perhaps Grace would be able to tell them what'd happened.

Jack dropped any trace of the TLC when he jabbed the answer button on his phone, and he put it on speaker. "Why the hell were you on that road just yards from where Scotty crashed?" Jack demanded.

Caroline had no trouble hearing Grace's sobs and broken breaths. "Scotty called me. He's dead, isn't he?"

"Yeah, he's dead," Jack snapped. If there'd been an award for good bedside manner, he would have lost big-time. There wasn't a trace of sympathy in his voice. "Now I want you to tell me who killed him."

"I honestly don't know," Grace answered through another sob. Caroline didn't think either the words or the crying was fake.

Jack didn't approve of that answer, and he showed that by swearing. "You need to go to the sheriff's office in Longview Ridge. As a minimum, you're a witness to a crime, but I'm betting you know a whole lot more than that."

"I don't!" Grace practically shouted. "And I'm not going to the cops. If a dirty lawman is doing this, I'll end up dead, just like Scotty. Maybe like Skylar and Nicola. Caroline might believe in you, but I don't, and personally, I think she's a fool to trust you."

With that, Grace ended the call.

Jack tried to call the woman back, of course, but neither of them was surprised when Grace didn't answer.

After he shoved his phone back in his pocket, his hands went on his hips, and his gaze fired to hers. Oh, the anger was there. A giant ball of it, and he didn't seem to know where to aim all that dangerous energy.

"Do you really think you're a fool to trust me?" Jack demanded.

He seemed to be throwing some kind of emotional gauntlet, and she thought that maybe he wouldn't be happy with any answer she gave him. So Caroline just stood there. Waiting. And watching the rising storm. Outside, the rain was now battering the windows. There was a crack of lightning. Thunder.

But the storm inside Jack seemed even more intense.

He turned away from her, but the temper had him whirling back around just as fast.

"You're an idiot, you know that?" Jack jabbed

his index finger at her. He wasn't shouting or touching her, but it was close. "I love you more than I've ever loved anything or anybody. Hell, I love you more than anyone's probably ever loved before. So believe it when I tell you that you can trust me. I wouldn't let a killer get near you. That includes someone in my own gene pool."

Caroline swallowed the lump in her throat. "You just called me an idiot."

He winced and somehow managed to make that expression look hot. "You noticed that, huh? I was hoping all the I-love-yous would gloss that over." His eyes went dark and serious. The color of storm clouds now. *"Believe it,"* he repeated, his voice a hoarse whisper.

She had no doubts—none—that the words came straight from his heart. "I believe it."

And since there'd been enough words, whispers and shouts, Caroline grabbed on to a handful of his shirt, eased him to her and showed him just how much she loved him right back.

With a kiss.

JACK HEARD HIMSELF say Caroline's name. It was more breath than sound, and he felt those tight muscles relax in his arms and chest. The relief came as his cheek pressed to hers with his mouth against her ear.

Of course, there would have been a whole lot more relief if she'd told him she loved him. But he could wait until she was ready. Believing in him was enough for now.

They stayed that way, standing there, for several long moments. He'd just taken her the night before, but the ache was already there as if he'd gone much too long without her. She was no doubt feeling some of that ache because she shifted, finding his mouth, and her kiss already had that hungry edge to it.

Jack understood the hunger.

He'd failed at being gentle with her before, and he could already feel a repeat of that. This time though, it was Caroline who was in the driver's seat, and it didn't seem as if she had *gentle* in mind.

"Your clothes are coming off," she said like an oath.

He wasn't about to argue with that, but he did have to get his eyes uncrossed when her hand slid down into his jeans and over his erection. He could hardly protest the maneuver since he'd done the same to her, but that bold move made him want their clothes off sooner than he'd planned.

Caroline pressed him face-first against the wall, like a cop making an arrest. "I can't think when you're kissing me," she said. "Your mouth should be classified as an illegal substance."

Jack got just a flash of male pride, which went to hell in a handbasket when she yanked off his holster. That went on the dresser. Not too long after that, his shirt landed on the floor.

Apparently, no area was off-limits for her, because Caroline's mouth went to the back of his neck, trailing down to his shoulders. Jack had never considered those to be parts of him that he wanted kissed, but it added a heap of fuel to the already blazing heat.

When he started to turn, to take her into his arms, she held him in place, using the lower part of her body and pressing him even harder against the wall. He felt her moving around, maneuvering, and then the touching continued.

While she kept up those long, lingering kisses, she slipped her hands around to his chest. Her fingers were as thorough as her mouth, and she traced each muscle to his stomach.

Then, lower.

She didn't slide her hand into his jeans this time. Instead, Caroline unzipped him, pushing both his jeans and the boxers off his hips, and she was damn clever doing it, too. And slow. Inch by slow inch. Her left hand skimmed over his butt while her right one took care of the front.

"Your body should be illegal, too," Caroline said in a breathy whisper that hit against his shoulder.

No time for male pride this time. Her fist slid the entire length of him. Then, that fist got even tighter. Her mouth—and yes, her tongue—continued on his shoulder, making slow circles and those maddening kisses.

Jack gritted his teeth and swallowed a groan. As good as it felt, and it felt damn good, he didn't want to finish things this way. He was about to tell Caroline that when she lowered his jeans and boxers and then used her foot to push them even farther down so that Jack could step out of them. The moment he did that, she took hold of his waist and spun him around.

Finally!

Or so he thought. But she dodged a kiss, stepping back from him. He could see the heat in her eyes. Hell, he could feel it. The air was firing between them like lightning bolts.

While facing him, she took hold of his hips, and walking backward, she led him to the bed. They stepped over his shirt, and that was when he saw her panties on the floor. He wasn't sure when she'd taken those off, maybe right before all that sanity-robbing touching when she'd had him against the wall.

Caroline reversed their positions when they

reached the bed, and pushed him onto the mattress. He landed on his back, and before he could even blink, she landed on him, straddling him.

The scalding kiss she gave him nearly had him forgetting that she still had on her clothes. Minus the panties. Jack got a quick reminder of it, though, when he finally got his hands on her, and he felt the barrier of her top and skirt. Her skirt had shifted up, though, so he could at least get one of his hands on her bare butt as he fumbled around to yank off her top.

But Caroline put an end to that, too. She levered up on her knees, and in the same motion, she took hold of him again. And then dropped so that he was inside her.

Jack didn't swallow the groan that time. Hell, it was possible his heart had skipped a whole bunch of beats. Pleasure roared through him. Caroline made sure that wasn't a solo thing, either. She shifted, riding him, taking everything he was more than willing to give her.

She found the rhythm. The right one that would wring out every drop of this, and just when she had him right at the brink, Jack reached between her legs to touch her, to give her a little boost to take her to climax with him. Before he could do that, though, she hauled him up to a sitting position so they were face-to-face.

The kiss came. It wasn't filled with hungry greed this time. This was gentle. Soft.

And whispering his name, Caroline wrapped her arms around him and finished them together.

Chapter Fourteen

Caroline didn't bother wondering if having sex with Jack was yet another mistake. It probably was. Loss of focus and all that. But she refused to regret what had happened and figured Jack was on the same page with her. He certainly wasn't doing anything to move her off him in the bed. In fact, he looked pleasured and satisfied.

It wouldn't last, though.

No. Not for her cowboy lawman.

Soon, very soon, he'd start to see the problems that this sort of intimacy would cause for the investigation. That didn't mean Jack didn't love her. He did. But clearly in his mind, this would put a little tarnish on his badge and a whole lot more tarnish on his judgment. It had to be hard to think straight when feelings ran this hot and deep for someone in his protective custody.

Hoping to stop his guilt trip before it started,

Caroline lifted her head and kissed Jack right on that incredible mouth of his. Rolling off him, she landed on her back next to him.

"Just remember that I'm the one who started this round," she said.

His breathing was still a little uneven when he turned on his side and looked at her. "I sure didn't do anything to stop you."

"It wouldn't have worked if you'd tried," Caroline assured him. "And that's all the whining we're allowed over this." She gave him another kiss—a quick, almost chaste one—and she forced herself off the bed. "I'm getting dressed so I can start doing computer checks and calls to look for Grace. Besides, Clarie might be wondering where we got off to."

"Clarie's smart," Jack grumbled. "She'll figure it out."

True, which would make it awkward when Jack and she came out of the bedroom and faced the deputy. Still, it had to be done because Clarie was no doubt working on the case, as well. She might not approve of them rolling around in the sack while she did the job.

Since her clothes were scattered everywhere, it meant traipsing around the room naked while she gathered them. Jack watched, of course, as if entertained by the peep show. But then he huffed, got up and started doing the same thing.

Caroline certainly got some entertainment of her own by seeing his incredible body flex and move, and she reminded herself that they wouldn't get any work done if she kept gawking at him.

"You do know we're going to have to do something, well, drastic, to draw our attacker out in the open?" she threw out there, knowing it would get his mind back where it needed to be.

Of course, he wouldn't like that word *drastic*, and Jack expressed that dislike with a scowl. Then a huff, which actually softened his expression. "Look, I know you're upset about Scotty's death, but—"

That was as far as he got with his protest before his phone rang. His jeans were still on the floor, so Jack had to rummage around to locate it.

Caroline didn't exactly breathe easier when she saw Kellan's name on the screen. That was because he could be calling with more bad news. She hurried to finish dressing in case Jack and she had to do something right away. Jack answered the call, and he put it on speaker.

"We got an ID on the dead gunman," Kellan said the moment he was on the line. "The name's probably not going to mean anything to you. Amos Treadwell. He's got a record and reputation for being a spine cracker for loan sharks and other lowlifes."

So just a hired gun. That did nothing to make her feel better about any of this, because a paid killer could have done just as much damage as the person who'd hired him, or more.

"Please tell me that you can link Treadwell to one of our suspects," Jack told his brother.

"I wish." Kellan sounded disgusted that he hadn't been able to do that. "But the CSIs did get something when they went through his pockets. Treadwell had other targets, and he'd written down the names on what he called his 'to-do list.'"

Caroline felt a fresh coil of fear slide through her. "What names?" she heard herself ask.

Kellan took his time answering, and that let her know she wasn't going to like what he was about to say. "Scotty, Grace, Jack, you and me."

No, she didn't like it, but it wasn't much of a surprise. At least the first four weren't, but she hadn't expected Kellan to be on that list. Obviously, neither had Jack, because his now tight jaw muscles went to war with each other.

"Why would Treadwell plan to kill you?" Jack demanded.

She had no trouble hearing the long breath that Kellan took before he answered. "The person who hired Treadwell probably thinks Caroline has spilled all by now and that you spilled it to me." Kellan paused, cursed. "The person could go after Gemma, too."

Or anyone else in Jack's family. That could include his partner, friends. The list could go on and on.

"I've put a reserve deputy on Gemma," Kellan added a moment later, "and I'm heading home right now. Eli and Owen are doing the same."

Caroline filled in the blanks on what Kellan *wasn't* saying. He couldn't keep this level of protection going for long. Eli and Owen had jobs to do along with their families to protect. Their attacker could just wait them out. Maybe wait even long enough until their guards were down and then go after them when they didn't expect it.

Mercy.

They had to do something, now, to put an end to it so they could all get on with their lives. Especially Owen and Eli, since their families included babies who needed protecting.

"I've been mulling over a plan," Caroline said.

As she'd expected, her comment caused some concern followed by anger to flash in Jack's eyes. She figured that if she could see Kellan, he'd have a similar expression. That meant she was going to have to do a hard sell to convince them that what she had in mind could work.

Probably.

But she would keep the word *probably* to herself. They'd have enough doubts without her adding more.

"Both of you know we need to do something to go ahead and draw out this person," Caroline continued. "Our attacker seems to believe that I know something. Something that would incriminate him or her. So why not put it out there that I'm remembering more details of what Eric said when he kidnapped me? I could be bait."

That, of course, didn't go over well. Jack cursed and shook his head. Kellan grumbled some of the same profanity.

"Just let me finish," she said, speaking over them. "Word could get out that I'm going to the Serenity Inn to meet with a therapist or counselor. Someone who can help me use the place to recall those final details that will help us figure out who Eric actually called that night and what he said to him or her."

"The killer won't go for that," Jack concluded, but she knew that he'd said that more out of worry for her than any doubt over the workability of the plan.

"He or she will, if word gets out," Caroline argued. "And we can use Grace to do that."

Jack huffed again. "Grace won't even answer her phone."

"No, but I'm pretty sure she'll read a text. We can ask her to leak that I'll be at the Serenity Inn. Tonight," she added, though Caroline cast an uneasy glance at the window. "If Grace is in on the plan to murder us, then she'll get the info to the right person. To the person who wants us dead. If she's innocent, then she can help us with the leak so we can lure out the killer."

The curtains and blinds were closed, but she could hear the rain battering against the glass. It wouldn't exactly be a good night to go to the old, abandoned hotel, but enduring the weather would be the least of their problems.

No huff from Jack this time, but he gave her a very flat look. "Our attacker could just send another hired thug."

Caroline nodded, knowing that was a strong possibility. The proof of that was the now dead gunman.

"We weren't expecting the other attacks," she explained, "but if we know this one is coming, we can be ready for it. Instead of killing any henchman who shows up, we can take him alive. Maybe shoot him with a tranquilizer gun instead of bullets. After we have him, we can make some kind of deal to get him to talk."

Jack certainly didn't jump on that, either, but she was hoping that once he got over his emotional objection, he would see it could work.

"What makes you think you can trust Grace?" Jack demanded. "What if she shows up and tries to kill you?"

"I'm not sure I can trust her, not completely, but that doesn't matter. If it's Grace who comes to the inn, then you can take her into custody and get her to tell you what she knows about Scotty's death." She paused. "But if she gets out the word, then the real killer or his hired gun might show up. It's worth a try."

Judging from the swear words that poured out of him, Jack didn't agree with her. "I don't want you at the inn," he snapped.

Caroline nodded, knowing he would say that. "I don't especially want to be there, either." Not with all the horrible things that had happened to her. There was the possibility of flashbacks. Heck, there was also the risk of a full-blown panic attack that would pretty much put her out of commission in a fight. "But we can't let this danger and the attacks go on."

"She's right about that," Kellan said before Jack could spout what would have almost certainly been more arguments. "It's dangerous for too many people. I can't protect everyone that this snake might target. He or she is desperate. That's obvious. Maybe because we're getting close to finding out what really happened that night Dad was murdered. A plan like this could be the tipping point to get us that truth."

"Yeah, and it could be the tipping point to getting Caroline shot," Jack fired back. But then he groaned.

Caroline went to him, looked him straight in the eyes. "This could end the danger in just a few hours," she reminded him. Then, she played dirty by adding, "We'd be able to get on with our lives."

Of course, Jack was ready for that to happen. Ready for them to be a couple again. To not have to look over their shoulders to make sure a hired gun didn't have them in his sight.

"Option two," she went on when Jack and Kellan didn't say anything. "I leave Longview Ridge. I disappear. Not through WITSEC or any other way that my location can be hacked or traced. And once I'm gone, none of you will be in danger."

Oh, that brought the storm straight back to Jack's narrowed eyes. "No," he said through clenched teeth. "I'm not losing you again."

Once more, it was exactly the answer she'd expected. Kellan voiced a version of the same by just saying, "You can forget doing that."

Caroline hadn't exactly expected them to agree. Nor did she want to leave Jack. But she'd offered it to give them a choice—which really wasn't a choice at all. So maybe now they'd see that her plan of using Grace was the only way to go.

Jack shook his head again. "What if we have Grace leak that you'll be at the inn first thing in the morning with the therapist? That would give us more time to get everything in place and maybe come up with something better." But almost immediately he waved that off. "It'd give the killer more time, too, and that's something we don't want."

"True." Caroline went even closer, until her body was right against his. "Jack, we need to text Grace and set this all up. We need to do this."

Silence was his reply, but despite it, she could practically hear Jack thinking. Trying to figure out a different way. One that didn't involve her. But other than her walking out of his life, he wouldn't be able to come up with anything that didn't put her in the mix.

Because she was at the center of it.

As long as she drew breath, the killer would come. Caroline just wanted that to happen on their terms and not the killer's.

"Well?" Kellan prompted when the silence dragged on.

Jack hesitated several more seconds before he scrubbed his hand over his face. "Okay. Let's get started."

JACK HAD SO many bad feelings about this, and those feelings came at him like a tornado. He didn't know which one he could latch on to and try to fix, because the whole plan was whirling around in his head and twisting up his insides.

The text had gone out to Grace, and the woman had actually responded right away, saying that she was on board with leaking the information, and that she wanted to help catch the person who'd murdered her friend Scotty. The woman assured them that she'd get the fake news to all three of their main suspects: Lily, Kingston and Zeller. That was good if the leak would actually lure out the killer or his hired gun. That was also good if they could trust Grace, but Jack wasn't sure on either of those counts.

Unlike Caroline.

He wasn't certain how she managed it, but she looked confident and as tough as nails. For the first time since she'd gotten back her memory, he didn't see fear in her eyes. Ironic, since this was the time when fear was plenty warranted. Too many unknowns. Too many things to go wrong. And here she could be within an hour of facing down someone who wanted her dead.

She sat across the dining room table from them, listening while Kellan went over the details. She wasn't nibbling on her bottom lip. Her hands weren't trembling. And she even gave Jack a smile when their gazes met.

Oh, man.

He hated putting Caroline in this position, and it was a potentially dangerous position despite Kellan's and his measures to keep her as safe as possible. One of those precautions was for her to wear a Kevlar vest beneath her clothes. Kellan, Clarie and he would, too, but that wasn't going to protect any of them if the killer or hired guns went with shots to the head. That was why once they arrived at the inn, they'd have to move fast to get Caroline inside.

Kellan's phone dinged with a text message, and he gave Jack a nod. "Gunnar says there's still no activity in or around the inn."

That wasn't a surprise, since the killer likely wouldn't have had time to get there yet. Unlike Gunnar and Deputy Manuel Garcia. Before Jack had even sent Grace the text, Manuel and Gunnar had gone to the inn to make sure it was vacant. That way, the killer couldn't get a jump on them and maybe set explosives or some other kind of trap.

Gunnar and Manuel had searched through each of the dilapidated rooms and around the grounds to make sure there'd be no surprises. After the two deputies had done that, they'd parked their vehicle on a hidden ranch trail where they could keep watch. They were armed with both tranq guns and their service weapons, with the tranquilizers being their first option so they could take the person alive. It wasn't foolproof—someone could still sneak by them on foot, but at least there would be backup nearby in case something went wrong.

And yes, there was a good chance something would indeed go wrong.

Kellan was right about the killer being desperate, and that increased the risk that the person might do something stupid. Stupid enough to try attacking Caroline with lawmen around. Jack didn't know exactly what the killer might do, but they had to be prepared for any-and everything.

At both Caroline's and Jack's insistence, Kellan would be going to his place with Gemma. No way did Jack want this plan to backfire and have the killer go after someone in his family and hold them hostage. That would give the killer plenty of bargaining power to try to get to Caroline.

"Are we ready to do this?" Caroline asked.

Jack couldn't come up with a reason to delay; they had to hurry this along. He wanted Caroline inside the inn before their attacker had a chance to get there first. Of course, if that did happen, then Gunnar would alert them, and Jack could get Caroline out of harm's way while they dealt with the snake that'd made their lives a living hell.

"Be safe," Kellan said, giving them one last look before he headed outside.

Jack didn't waste any time. He grabbed his equipment bag and got Caroline and Clarie out to the cruiser. The rain had slacked up some, but he'd checked the forecast and knew they could get drizzle on and off all night. He doubted that would keep a killer away, but it would make things uncomfortable for Gunnar and Manuel, who were outside in this weather.

"This is your last chance to change your mind," Jack told Caroline the moment they were in the cruiser.

She immediately shook her head. "You know this is something we have to do."

He wasn't sure of that at all. Yes, he was well aware that the threats couldn't continue. Especially since the dead gunman had been planning on going after Kellan and Grace. The person who'd paid him for that could just turn around and hire someone else to carry through on that to-do list.

Clarie drove, and Jack sat with Caroline in the back seat. Even though it was nearly dark now, he continued to keep watch. They'd also had a couple of the ranch hands patrol the road to make sure no one had pulled off or was lying in wait for them.

More precautions.

And Jack took yet one more. He slid a backup weapon from his equipment bag and handed it to Caroline. If he'd seen any indications that she wasn't comfortable with the gun, he would have rethought his offer. But she took it right away.

"Obviously, it's not a tranq gun," he explained, "but you might need it if someone gets past Gunnar and Manuel."

"Thanks," she said. "By the way, I do know how to use it, and Lucille taught me a lot of self-defense moves."

Hell, he prayed it didn't come down to that, and he forced himself to believe that the best-case scenario would happen. That their attacker would rush to the inn and they could catch him or her.

Even though it was only a few miles, it seemed to take an eternity to get to the inn, and Jack's concerns continued to snowball with each passing second. However, he didn't see or hear anything to make him tell Clarie to turn around and go back to the ranch.

When Clarie reached the inn, she pulled up as close as she could to the wide front porch, and Jack leaned down a little so he could look up at the place. Once it had been a mansion.

A showcase for someone who'd had lots and lots of money. When the rich owner had passed away, his heirs had turned it into an inn, a business that had ultimately failed, and they'd let it go when they couldn't pay the taxes. So it had stood abandoned, empty and neglected for years. That was why there was definitely nothing welcoming about it now.

"Talk about creepy," Clarie grumbled.

Yeah, that was the right word for it. Most of the windows had been boarded up, and the ones that hadn't been were just dark holes of jagged, broken glass.

The grounds hadn't fared much better with time and lack of care. Once, there'd been gardens, but now it was an overgrown jumble of trees, underbrush and weeds. Some vines coiled out from that tangle and had snaked their way up the brick-and-stone facade.

Caroline was studying the place, too, but Jack figured it was more than just creepy for her. It was the place of her own personal nightmares. Where she'd come too darn close to dying over a year ago, when Eric had kidnapped her and brought her here.

After Jack gave Clarie a nod, the three of them got out and hurried up the steps and inside. Nothing was welcoming here, either. Just an empty shell with scarred wood floors and walls with holes and graffiti.

Broken glass was scattered everywhere, and they would hopefully use that to their advantage. When Gunnar and Manuel had gone through the place, they'd kicked up piles of it next to all the doors and the unboarded windows. That way, if an intruder came in, they should be able to hear when he or she stepped on the shards.

Since the killer was supposed to believe that Caroline was there to meet a therapist, Jack and Clarie started setting the scene. He stayed right by Caroline's side while he took out the flashlights. Not for them to carry. No, he would put these in the foyer and the adjoining room so it would seem as if that was where they were.

It wouldn't be.

"This way," Jack said, leading Caroline and Clarie away from the lights.

The plan was to take them to the first room off the hall behind the winding staircase, but Caroline stopped and glanced down.

There was a bloodstain on the foyer floor.

Not fresh, thank God.

Nor was it Caroline's.

It belonged to Gemma, who'd also been attacked here over a year ago. The memory of his father, who had been murdered that night, gave Jack another sucker punch of grief. Even though Gemma had survived the attack, seeing that bloodstain brought it all back, and he was certain it was even worse for Caroline. She'd nearly been killed that night, too.

Jack pushed that all aside and got them moving to the room where they'd wait this out. It wasn't ideal since it did have a window, but at least this one was boarded up. Plus, if things went to hell in a handbasket, they could move into one of the other dozen or so rooms that fed off the hall.

The three of them stood there a moment so their eyes could adjust to the near darkness. Some of the milky light from the foyer made its way here. Just enough to create some spooky shadows and show dust motes floating like little ghosts around the room.

It was no wonder that some folks called the place haunted and only came here when dares, too much alcohol or both played into the mix.

"There's a blanket in the equipment bag," he told Caroline, knowing she wasn't going to use it. She didn't.

Caroline went to the window with Clarie, each taking a side so they could peer out through the cracks in the boards. Jack took up position by the door so he could see not only the hall but the front door.

And the wait began.

Even though Grace had gotten out the "leak" fast, it didn't mean their attacker had managed to get things ready to come to the inn. But that thought had no sooner crossed his mind when his phone dinged with a text message. A message that had Jack cursing under his breath.

"Gunnar spotted someone on the road," Jack relayed to Caroline and Clarie. "The person's on foot and headed our way."

Chapter Fifteen

Caroline forced herself to breathe normally. Well, as normally as she could manage, considering this was possibly the showdown that she'd been preparing herself for.

And the one that she'd feared.

She wasn't immune to the panic that wanted to explode inside her, but she reminded herself that this was necessary. It would be impossible for her to put the past behind her if she was still dealing with it. And she felt in her gut that the attacks were connected to her past.

Specifically, to Eric.

Either someone thought Eric had spilled secrets to her, or else they were just tying up loose ends that they believed Eric had left behind. Lily and Zeller fit with the first theory. Kingston with the second.

"Did Gunnar spot a man or woman?" Caroline asked Jack. Even though she whispered her question, it practically echoed in the empty room.

"He's not sure." Jack whispered, too, but there was an angry edge to his voice. "Gunnar said he only got a glimpse of someone dressed all in black before the person ducked off the road and into some trees."

There were certainly a lot of trees, and they dotted the landscape all the way from the road to what was left of the old gardens surrounding the inn. Someone could use them for cover, but eventually the attacker would have to come out into the open to make it inside.

Well, maybe.

It was possible to get into the house by crawling through the underbrush at the back, but it would still take some maneuvering.

"You want me to move to one of the front rooms so I can try to see this person?" Clarie asked.

Jack stayed quiet a moment, obviously giving her question some thought. "No. Gunnar and Manuel have good positions. They should be able to see if anyone approaches the inn, and if need be, one of them can move closer to get a better shot with the tranq gun."

Caroline knew it was the *should be* that was eating away at Jack. He wanted absolutes when it came to her safety, but that wasn't going to happen. The best they could do right now was to have a good shot at putting an end to this.

"What kind of range is there on the tranq gun they're using?" Clarie asked a moment later.

"They actually have tranq rifles, and the range on those is supposed to be 210 feet. But Gunnar didn't think it was smart to risk a shot that far out. He'll want closer."

Caroline agreed with that. It wouldn't be like firing an automatic or semiautomatic, and if they missed on the first shot, they'd have to manually reload. That could give the person time to get away. However, Kellan had assured them that Gunnar and Manuel were both good marksmen with steady hands. And if they failed, then they'd go for a nonkill shot with their regular weapons.

There was also a possible problem with the tranq itself. It wouldn't have an instant effect, and it could take several minutes to incapacitate the person. Still, the drug should make it a whole lot harder for their visitor to try to kill them. Plus, as soon as Gunnar or Manuel fired the tranq, they'd move in to apprehend.

"Zeller's stupid if he doesn't smell a trap," Jack muttered just loud enough for Caroline to hear.

That, too, wasn't setting well with him. Jack didn't want to think of a fellow lawman being at the center of this, but it was possible. Zeller had the means and opportunity. He had a possible motive, as well, if he was trying to cover up his involvement in the sex-trafficking ring.

But Jack was right that Zeller should be able to smell a trap.

After all, the marshal had personal knowledge of her case and had almost certainly gone over every record of hers that existed. He might know that there were no other memories for her to recover. However, she was hoping he had enough doubts about her, about what she'd possibly remembered, that he would take the risk of coming here.

Of course, it was just as likely that he could have hired someone to do his dirty work, but she didn't want to think about that now. If Zeller was guilty, he would come, and then Jack could arrest him.

Caroline peeked out through the sliver of space in between the boards and tried to get a glimpse of this possible attacker. Nothing. She could definitely see some trees and vines, but not a person. Listening didn't help, either, because the only things she could clearly hear were the patter of the rain and her own heartbeat in her ears.

Jack's phone dinged again, the sound shooting through the room and nearly causing Caroline to gasp. Clearly, she didn't have her emotions under control as much as she wanted.

"It's from Gunnar," Jack said after giving Caroline a quick look. No doubt to make sure she was still okay. Just because she hadn't gasped out loud, it didn't mean Jack hadn't sensed her nerves. "He got another glimpse of the person, and he's pretty sure it's a woman."

Maybe it was Lily, and if so, it meant she hadn't sent a henchman but planned on doing the job herself. Of course, that didn't mean the woman didn't have hired guns in the area.

"Gunnar couldn't tell if the woman was armed," Jack went on, reading the text. She saw him click the button to set his phone to vibrate, probably so the killer wouldn't be alerted by the sound of any other incoming messages. "But she just ducked into some oaks on the east side of the inn."

Caroline wasn't exactly sure which way east was, but she turned her attention back to the window in case the woman came that way. Behind her, she heard the soft clicks of Jack texting.

"I told Gunnar to try to get closer to the woman so he can take her or get a better shot," Jack explained. "But Manuel's staying in place so he has a bird's-eye view of the house and grounds. This person might be a decoy, and I don't want someone else sneaking up on us."

A decoy would definitely be something their

attacker would try. He or she had never come at them head-on and likely wouldn't want to do that now. The person was basically a coward, and that played into the mental profile she'd done. So yes, they needed to expect some kind of trickery or deception, and with the sprawling grounds around the inn, this woman could be drawing their attention while someone—maybe another hired gun—slipped closer to them.

She looked over her shoulder and saw Jack move out of the doorway and glance toward both ends of the hall. He must not have seen or heard anything suspicious, because he stepped back in.

Caroline looked outside again, trying to pick through the darkness and the rain. Willing herself to see something.

And she did.

Thanks to a bolt of lightning, Caroline saw the blur of motion next to one of the massive oaks.

"Did you see that?" Clarie immediately asked.

"I did." And Caroline was almost positive that it was a woman. One who was no longer in sight.

"Clarie, switch places with me for a second," Jack told the deputy, and Clarie immediately hurried across the room to take up position by the door as Jack came to the window.

"She's behind the center tree in that cluster," Caroline explained, motioning in the direction where she'd spotted the person. "I didn't get a look at her face, but I think she's wearing a ski mask."

Which would make sense. Not only would it conceal her identity, but it would make her face less likely to stand out in the darkness. Ditto for the black clothes. If it hadn't been for the lightning, Caroline might have missed the figure.

Jack continued to keep watch. Waiting. And Mother Nature cooperated with another lightning flash. It lit up the area by the trees for just a second. Enough for them to see that no one was there. Either the woman had moved or she had stayed behind cover.

Caroline soon got the answer as to which had happened.

Despite the rain and her own ragged breath, Caroline heard the sound. So did Jack and Clarie. Their heads whipped up in its direction. It had come not from the trees but rather the back of the inn. And it was something they'd been listening for.

The sound of someone stepping on broken glass.

An intruder was inside the house.

JACK SILENTLY CURSED, bracing himself for a fight. He'd known all along that it would be possible for someone to get in the house without the deputies or anyone else seeing them, but he had hoped that wouldn't happen. Now that it had, he needed to do something about it.

He motioned for Clarie to switch places with him again and for her and Caroline to stay in place at the window. That would accomplish two things. The women could continue to keep watch in case this intruder was a decoy, and Caroline would keep out of the most probable line of fire.

Because Jack was certain the person who'd just stepped on that glass would soon be heading to the lights in the foyer.

Clarie took out her phone to send a text to Gunnar. It was part of the plan they'd worked out while still back at his house. She would let Gunnar know about the problem, and then either Gunnar or Manuel would move in closer to assist. The other would stay back to watch for anyone else.

Jack didn't move. Not yet. He just stood there, waiting for the next sound, and he didn't have to wait long.

More footsteps.

At first, those footsteps crunched over the broken glass, but then that stopped. It didn't mean the intruder had left or had even quit moving. It only meant the glass was no longer in the path to alert Jack.

Dragging in a long breath, Jack tightened his grip on his gun and leaned slightly out the doorway so they could start the next phase of this trap. After all, they'd lured the killer or a henchman here with the news that Caroline was trying to recover all her memories. It was best if he played along with that for now.

"Just take a deep breath, Caroline," he said, trying to make it seem as genuine as possible. "Try to clear your mind and think about what else you heard in that phone call. What did the caller say to Eric?"

With his lines delivered, he motioned for Caroline to jump into this.

"I'm okay." Caroline's shaky voice definitely didn't mesh with the strong woman who was keeping watch out the window. "And I do think I remember. Yes, I can hear the person speaking…"

She purposely let her words trail off. Also as planned.

Jack listened for more of the footsteps. Nothing. But Clarie gave him the thumbs-up to indicate that one of the deputies was moving closer to the house. Since Jack hadn't heard her phone ding with the message, Clarie had likely silenced it.

"Can you tell if it's a man or woman talking to Eric?" Jack asked to keep his therapy conversation going with Caroline.

Again, she mumbled her response, but she strung it out for a few seconds. Hopefully, the intruder would think she was having some kind of revelation and would get there fast to try to silence her. Jack didn't want this dragging on any longer than necessary, and he could stop the person as soon as she came into view.

"There's someone else out there," Caroline whispered.

Even though her voice had been barely loud enough for him to hear, those words roared through his head. "Is it Gunnar?" he mouthed.

"No. Someone else. I think it's the same woman I saw before. She's still out there by the trees."

So that meant it was a henchman in the house, so maybe the fake therapy conversation with Caroline didn't matter. If this thug had orders to kill, then he wouldn't care what they were saying. Wouldn't care if Caroline remembered anything or not, since the plan was for her to be dead soon.

Jack wasn't going to let that plan happen.

Clarie sent another text. Probably to Gunnar again so she could give him a heads-up. No way did they want the deputy walking into an ambush, since the woman by the tree could gun him down. Of course, Gunnar would be looking for exactly that sort of thing.

Jack finally heard another footstep, closer this time, and he considered doing more of the fake conversation with Caroline. He decided against it, though, in case the intruder could use his voice to pinpoint their location in the house.

Another footstep. Then another. The person was coming closer, and Jack knew it wouldn't be long before the person made it to the foyer. It seemed to him that the intruder was making a beeline toward those flashlights.

"The woman outside is moving," Caroline whispered. "And I see Gunnar."

Jack wasn't sure if that was a good thing or not. Certainly Gunnar had gotten Clarie's warning, but the deputy might not have seen the woman.

Or she might have seen him.

Jack considered having Clarie send Gunnar another warning text, but it was too risky with the intruder this close to them. And the person was indeed close. Even though there were no more footsteps, Jack could hear some kind of movement. Maybe he or she was getting his or her own weapon ready to launch the attack.

It felt as if everything went still. As if everyone and everything were holding their breath. Waiting for something to happen.

And it did.

There was a plinking sound. Something metal had dropped to the floor.

At first, Jack wondered if the intruder had let something slip and fall. Maybe his weapon. But he soon realized that it wasn't an accident.

Jack caught the first scent of the tear gas.

Chapter Sixteen

Caroline had had no trouble hearing the sound of something falling on the old wood floor of the inn. But she didn't know what it was and had no idea what had suddenly put that troubled look on Jack's face.

But she soon found out.

"Tear gas," Clarie managed to say at the exact moment the deputy began coughing.

Almost immediately, Caroline felt her eyes, nose and throat start to burn, and if it truly was tear gas, she figured it wouldn't be long before it basically incapacitated them. It wouldn't knock them unconscious, but they wouldn't be able to fight if they couldn't breathe. If they couldn't see.

And it was quickly getting to that point.

"This way," Jack snapped, and he tipped his head toward the hall. He had his left arm crooked and pressed to his face while he continued to grip his weapon in his right hand.

Both Caroline and Clarie rushed away from the window and toward him. When she looked out into the hall, she saw the wisps of the white fog. Yes, definitely tear gas. And as bad as it was right now, they weren't getting the full impact yet. That fog was rolling their way.

But where was the intruder who'd likely set all of this in motion?

She didn't see any signs of anyone, but it was possible the person had put on a gas mask. If so, he or she could come through that fog after them.

Jack's eyes had to be burning like fire—hers certainly were—but his gaze still slashed all around. A few seconds crawled by, and then he motioned for Clarie and her to follow him. The three of them barreled out into the hall with Jack in front of her and Clarie behind.

They ran fast but didn't go far, only a couple of yards, before Jack ducked into one of the other rooms, and he shut the door behind them. Caroline soon saw why he'd chosen this one. There were no boards on the window, something he'd probably learned from Gunnar and Manuel when they'd done their initial search of the place. No boards would mean both easy access for an intruder and escape for them.

Jack hurried to the window and threw it open. "Keep watch," he said, his voice rough and raw.

Caroline knew there was a good possibility that a would-be killer was waiting for them out there. That could have been part of the plan all along. Get them out so they could be gunned down. But the primal part of her brain was screaming for her to escape from the tear gas and get some fresh air.

Jack went out the window first. The moment his feet were on the ground, he glanced around again. He was looking for anyone who might be there to attack, but in the same motion, he took hold of Caroline's arm. He pulled her out with him, pushing her against the side of the inn. Keeping in front of her to protect her.

She dragged in a long, much-needed breath. Then another. And she blinked hard to clear away the remnants of the tear gas. The rain helped, but her eyes were still stinging and she couldn't see clearly.

Clarie climbed out of the window then, landing on her feet right next to Caroline, but they didn't stay put. Maybe because Jack believed the intruder would be coming to that room, to that window.

Keeping close to the wall, they hurried through the weeds and underbrush. It wasn't easy. The ground was soft from the rain, and Caroline's shoes bogged in the mud while the bushes scraped and poked at her. Still, it was better than being in there with the tear gas.

They ran, weaving in and out of the ground clutter until they were at the edge of the porch that stretched all the way across the front of the inn. They dropped down next to what was left of the porch railing. Not far from the cruiser. But to get to it, they'd have to go out into the open.

"Stay down," Jack whispered to her, and he maneuvered Caroline behind one of the overgrown shrubs while he peered around the corner at the porch. "I don't see anyone," he added.

Good. Maybe they'd get a few minutes to regroup and recover. They desperately needed that, and then maybe they could pinpoint the location of the person who'd gone inside.

As her eyes and mind started to clear, Caroline got a horrible thought. What if the person was already gone? It was possible that he or she had already escaped, maybe because they believed the tear-gas ploy had failed. If so, then Jack and she were right back where they started—without any proof as to who wanted her dead.

"I'll text Gunnar and let him know our location," Clarie whispered, taking out her phone.

While she did that, Caroline got as good of a grip as she could manage on the gun that Jack had given her. Even though her hand was weak, she needed to be able to help if it came down to a fight, and everything inside her said that was exactly what was going to happen.

"Gunnar lost sight of the woman by the trees," Clarie relayed when she got a response to her text. "He's going to look for her while he makes his way here to us."

Caroline welcomed the backup, but she knew it would also pose a big problem. They wouldn't be able to fire if they heard or saw something, because they wouldn't want to risk hitting Gunnar. Plus, this meant Manuel was alone and without backup. The deputy wouldn't be a primary target for the attacker, but he was still at risk.

Jack glanced back at her, their gazes connecting for a moment, and she saw the fear on his face. Not fear for himself but for her. Caroline wished she could do something to assure him that it would be okay, but she wasn't certain it would be.

And that cut to the bone.

Once again, Jack was in trouble because of her.

Maybe she should have just gone off on her own, far away from him. But while that would have been the smart thing to do, it would have crushed both their hearts. She didn't want him hurt, or worse, but at least they were together.

"I'm going to get in the cruiser and drive it over here," Jack said. "I'll get as close as I can. Wait here with Caroline," he added to Clarie.

But Caroline was already shaking her head before he even finished. "You can't go out there. If this person had tear gas, you know he'll have a gun. He'll be watching the cruiser."

Jack didn't disagree with any of that. He couldn't. However, the look he gave her let her know that he was going to do it anyway. Maybe because he felt it was the only option they had.

"We can wait for Gunnar," Caroline tried, though it wasn't much of an argument. They could be attacked before the deputy made it to them, and he had his hands full looking for the woman. If they managed to capture her, it could possibly give them as many answers as catching the person who'd used that tear gas on them.

Jack levered himself up, and he gave her one last look. A dozen things passed between them. A silent conversation that Caroline wished she could have said aloud.

She had so many things to say to him.

"Be careful" was the only thing she managed before he moved away.

Keeping low, Jack left the meager cover of the shrubs and started for the cruiser. Like their trek from the window, it wouldn't be easy. He'd have to deal with the soggy ground along with the rocks and tangled underbrush.

Clarie moved in front of her, protecting her as Jack had done, but Caroline kept her eyes on Jack until he disappeared behind what was left of a hedge. She maneuvered herself up so she could try to see him, and that was when she heard the sound behind her.

Caroline pivoted, bringing up her gun.

But it was already too late.

JACK WAS ONLY a few yards away from the cruiser when the front door of the inn opened and the tear-gas canister came shooting out.

Hell. Not again.

He only got a glimpse of the person who'd launched it, someone wearing black clothes and a mask. But whoever it was immediately stepped back, using the darkness and the white cloud of gas to hide behind.

"Caroline," Jack said on an oath. He couldn't see Clarie or her, but he figured this was some kind of ploy to get to her.

And it could work.

Jack had a fast debate with himself about getting into the cruiser so he could use it to get closer to the women and give them some cover. But with the uneven ground and some large landscape rocks, he could get stuck. If that happened, he might be too late to save them.

Cursing, he turned around and started running to get back to them, but the gas stung at his eyes like acid. Plus, even though he'd only gotten a few whiffs of it, he was already finding it hard to breathe. It had to be a lot worse for Caroline and Clarie. They were right there, next to where the canister had gone off, so they were no doubt getting the brunt of it.

With that thought racing through his head, Jack cut through the same shrubs and weeds he'd just trampled through so he could make his way back to them. He seriously doubted that their attacker had simply tossed that canister just to make them more miserable than they already were. No. This was some kind of ploy— Jack could feel that in his gut.

He could hear the women coughing. That was a good sign because it meant they were alive, but their instincts would be to run. To get as far away from the gas as possible. That would take them out into the open where they could be gunned down, and they wouldn't even be able to see their attacker.

Jack tried to keep watch around him. Hard to do, but he kept pressing. Kept moving. And his heart went to his knees when he reached the side of the porch and didn't see either Caroline or Clarie. They'd moved.

But where?

The weather didn't cooperate as he listened for them. The sky unzipped, the rain pounding down on him, making it hard to hear. It would clear the air, but it wouldn't happen nearly fast enough.

Jack kept running, and he finally heard the coughing again. No sounds of a struggle with a would-be killer, thank God, and he needed to make it to them to keep it that way.

He stayed close to the wall of the inn, but that meant checking each window to make sure he wasn't about to be ambushed when he went past it. He didn't see anyone. That was the good news. The bad news was that Caroline and Clarie had likely moved to the back of the building.

From where the intruder had gotten inside.

The person could be there, waiting.

Caroline and Clarie were armed, he reminded himself, and he hung on to that thought while he kept moving.

Now it was the rain that was stinging his eyes, and somehow the tear gas was still making its way to him. There was some gas coming out of the inn, too, which Jack discovered when he hurried past the window where Clarie, Caroline and he had escaped the first canister.

Even though he doubted they would go back inside with that tear-gas fog, he made a quick glimpse inside.

No one.

He could no longer hear any coughing or other sounds of movement, and he hoped that was a good sign. That Clarie and Caroline had managed to find some clear air and a safe place to take cover.

Jack considered texting Clarie to let her know he was nearby, but he decided against that. If they were hiding from an attacker, he didn't want to give away their location. Besides, Clarie knew that Gunnar was also out here, somewhere, so she wouldn't pull the trigger without making sure it wasn't one of them.

He took another step and cursed when he nearly tripped over something. Not something, Jack quickly realized.

Someone.

It was a woman, and she was in a crumpled heap at his feet.

That sent his heart rate into a gallop, and he felt the cold fear ripple over his skin. No. Please. Not Caroline.

Jack dropped to his knees, and he forced himself to rein in his emotions. At least he tried to do that. It was nearly impossible to think of the woman he loved being hurt. Or worse. To think of her dead.

But it wasn't Caroline.

He could see that once he managed to wipe the rain from his eyes so he could get a better look. It was Clarie. And she was breathing. Thank God for that, but she wasn't okay. There was blood on her head and in her hair, and since there was a metal pipe next to her, Jack assumed that was the weapon that'd been used to assault her.

Where was Caroline?

Jack's gaze fired all around, but he didn't see her, and everything inside him was telling him he had to get to her now. Still, he sent a quick text to Gunnar to let the deputy know Clarie's location and that she needed medical help—fast. He hated leaving her there alone, but whoever had done this to her now had Caroline. Jack was sure of that.

Using his forearm to push aside the sopping wet shrubs, Jack hurried toward the back of the inn. He tried to listen for any sounds she might make. But he heard nothing. That certainly didn't tamp down his fears.

When his phone vibrated with a text message, he glanced down at the screen and saw Gunnar's response. I'm on my way to Clarie now.

Good. That would be one less thing on Jack's

mind, but he said a quick prayer that Clarie's injuries wouldn't be critical. With an attacker on the loose, it could be a while before they could get an ambulance in here for her.

Jack pushed through another cluster of overgrown shrubs, and he finally saw the edge of the back porch. The pressure clamped around his heart, though, when there was still no sign of Caroline. Hell. Had the person who'd tossed that tear gas managed to get away with her in tow?

He plowed his way through more of the weeds, and running now, he made it to the porch.

And there she was.

Not alone.

Not safe, either.

Caroline was on the porch, and despite the darkness, Jack could see that the color had drained from her face. With good reason. Because there was someone standing behind her.

Someone with a knife to her throat.

"I'm sorry," Caroline said. There was a trickle of blood running down the side of her head and more blood on her sleeve. "Because of the tear gas, I didn't see him in time."

Jack pushed aside her apology for something that wasn't her fault, and he focused on the "him" who was holding Caroline. Definitely a man. Jack could tell from his size despite most of his body being concealed. The coward was hiding behind Caroline.

Who was it?

Was it just another hired gun who'd been sent to kill them?

Jack couldn't tell, because the guy was wearing a gas mask. Not for long, though. Using his free hand, he peeled off the mask, tossing it onto the porch, and flashed a smile.

"Hello, Jack," Kingston said. "Caroline and I have been waiting for you."

FROM THE MOMENT Kingston had come out of the shadows and clubbed Clarie on the head, Caroline had known it would come down to this. Kingston wanted her dead, but he hadn't killed her when he'd hit her with the metal pipe because he'd first wanted to use her to lure out Jack. Kingston wouldn't have been able to use a dead woman to get himself in a position to murder both Jack and her.

And it had worked.

Jack had a gun, and to the best of her knowledge, Kingston only had a knife now that he'd discarded the pipe, but Jack wouldn't have a clean shot with Kingston using her as a human shield.

"Is Clarie all right?" she asked, hating that her voice shook when she spoke. She didn't want to give Kingston any more satisfaction from this, and hearing the fear in her voice probably added to his sick enjoyment.

But why was he doing this?

Caroline hoped she could learn that before she got out of this dangerous situation. And she would get out. There were so many lives at risk—Jack, Clarie, Caroline herself and the deputies outside. No way was she just going to let this piece of slime kill them. First, though, she'd need to get away from that knife he was holding. It was sharp—she knew that because he'd already cut her arm to prove that—and now he had it against her jugular.

"Clarie's fine," Jack said before he shifted his attention to Kingston. Jack's eyes narrowed, and his expression was hard as steel. "Let me guess. You're doing some favors for your old friend Eric."

"I am," Kingston readily admitted, and yes, he was enjoying this. He wanted them to know what he was doing and why. "Last year, Eric called me right from this inn while he was holding Caroline, and he asked me to tie up any and all loose ends for him. Ta-da! That's what I'm doing."

She didn't recall that conversation because she'd been drugged, but hearing what Kingston had just said caused the anger to roar through her. Caroline had to force herself not to ram Kingston in the gut with her elbow. They needed more info from him. Because Jack and she had their own loose ends to tie up. Yes, they would stop Kingston and arrest him, but when that happened, he might clam up. They had to know if others were involved in this.

"Kingston hired Scotty to hack into WITSEC and find my location," Caroline said. She didn't have proof of that, but considering the circumstances, that was a good guess. "It wasn't very smart of you to show up at my house, though."

"Of course, it was," Kingston immediately argued. "Me being there, it made me look innocent."

It had. Well, in a way. But Kingston had always been one of their top suspects.

"And after you were done with Scotty, you hired thugs to kill him," Jack said.

Jack moved a little to his left, and Caroline felt the pressure of the blade against her throat. "That's a no-no. Stay put, Marshal, or I cut her before I'm ready."

It turned her stomach to hear him say he was going to kill her no matter what. That made it even more important to draw this out. Because Jack wasn't the only lawman out there. Gunnar and Manuel were here, too. Maybe one of them could get into position to take Kingston out.

"Scotty was a loose end," Kingston went on a moment later. "So is Caroline, but she's been a little slippery when it comes to finishing up things. I thought it would be a nice touch to kill her here. Eric would appreciate that."

"Eric was a manipulative sociopath," Caroline spat out. "The only things he enjoyed were using people and killing. He used you, Kingston."

"Maybe because I wanted to be used."

That was almost certainly the truth. He was as twisted as Eric.

"The person who talked to Eric on the phone that night used cop jargon," she threw out there a moment later.

"Yes, a nice touch. That was Eric's idea. He wanted to play with your head, maybe make you think he was talking to Jack."

That gave her another jolt of anger, and she could see that it'd done the same to Jack. It was too late to punish Eric for that, but they sure as heck could make Kingston pay for his part in it.

She had to pause and gather her breath. "Who else did Eric and you use? Zeller or Lily? How about Grace?"

"None of the above." Again, no hesitation, but Caroline wasn't sure it was true.

Apparently, Jack wasn't convinced of it, either. "You're sure one of them didn't help you?"

"Nope. Me and me alone. Well, other than those two incompetent idiots I hired. Amos Treadwell was supposed to shoot you. He failed. Jessa Monroe was the woman who threw the first tear-gas canister. She panicked and tried to run so I killed her."

Caroline didn't like having another dead body added to this, but she was glad Jessa wasn't around to give her boss any help.

"And that's why I'm doing this myself. Oh, but I did get Scotty to set up Zeller," Kingston added. "You know, by planting that tracking device on his computer. All smoke, I assure you, since Scotty had already hacked in and gotten the address."

Caroline figured Scotty had done all of that for money. Lots of it, which Kingston could have gotten his hands on. Scotty probably hadn't figured the hacking would get him killed.

"And Lily?" Jack pressed. Like her, he must have decided to get all they could from Kingston.

"Nothing to do with me, but I had Scotty do some hacking in her files, too, and she was a naughty girl. Very involved in the sex trafficking. Tell you what. You can have those files for free. Just get them from my computer in my home office. I've got her bank records and some personal emails. There should be enough there for you to convict her of multiple crimes."

"Enough to convict her of murder?" Jack snapped.

"No. Not that." He stopped. "Oh, I see. You think Lily might have murdered that woman, Nicola, and your dad. Nope. Lily scared some woman into disappearing, but she didn't kill anyone."

"Skylar's alive?" Caroline managed to say.

"Alive and in hiding. If Lily had gotten to her, I would have heard about it. And it was Eric who did Nicola. Don't know the full story on that, but their paths crossed."

So, Skylar hadn't been murdered after all, and once Lily was behind bars, Skylar would likely surface. It didn't surprise Caroline that Eric had killed Nicola, but there was a huge piece of this that didn't fit.

"Eric didn't kill Jack's father," she said. "I was with Eric when Buck Slater was gunned down."

Caroline couldn't see Kingston's expression, but she could see Jack. His eyes went dark, and she could feel the dangerous edge whipping off him. And she knew why. Kingston was almost certainly smiling.

Because he'd been the one to kill Jack's father.

"Eric needed a distraction," Kingston said.

"He wanted gunfire to draw the attention off him so he could get away."

Her knees nearly buckled. The weight was so heavy on her chest that it felt as if someone was crushing her heart in a tight fist. And despite all of that, Caroline knew what she was feeling was a drop in the bucket compared to Jack. He'd just listened to the man responsible for his father's murder dismiss it as a mere distraction.

Caroline tried to give Jack a steadying look. A silent "calm down" because she didn't want the rage overtaking him so that he charged at Kingston. They just needed more time. Time that maybe she could buy them.

"You can't think you'll get away with this," she said to Kingston.

"Depends on what you mean by getting away with it." She felt his shoulder move in what she thought might be a shrug. The arrogant SOB. "With my lawyers, I doubt very seriously that I'll be declared competent or sane enough to stand trial. And my psychiatric records will prove it."

Records that Kingston had likely doctored. Or else Scotty had done that for him. But Jack and she could try to use his confession to prove otherwise. And even if they couldn't, he would still spend the rest of his life locked up in a mental institution. Not exactly justice, but it would have to do.

Caroline finally saw what she'd been looking for. Gunnar. He crept in behind one of the shrubs near Jack. Kingston must have seen him, too, but he didn't react. Probably because Gunnar didn't have any better angle of a shot than Jack did.

"Once Caroline's dead, there'll be no more loose ends," Kingston announced, and the muscles in his arm and hand tightened. He was going to do it.

Kingston was going to kill her.

Caroline was going to make sure that didn't happen. Gathering her breath, she directed her anger and fear to her voice and let out a vicious shout as she rammed her elbow into Kingston. She dropped her weight, getting her neck away from that knife. She felt it cut her again, on the side of her head, but she ignored that and scrambled away from Kingston.

Jack moved in. As fast and as mean as a snake.

Caroline had managed to get only a few feet away before Jack was on the porch. He kicked away the knife.

And tossed his gun aside.

When Kingston lunged at him, Jack went after the man with his fists, and Jack was a lot better at it than Kingston. He rammed his fist into Kingston's face, causing the man's head to flop back. Jack hit him again. And again. His fists pounding Kingston even as the man dropped to his knees on the porch. Jack might have kept it up, but Caroline touched his shoulder.

"Let Gunnar arrest him," she said, trying to keep her voice as calm as possible.

Caroline wasn't sure that would be enough to get Jack to stop.

But it was.

Jack froze, his fist still poised midair and aimed at Kingston's face. Kingston was crying now, his breath coming out in wet, loud sobs. Jack stared at the man several long moments before he stepped back. Caroline was right there to pull Jack into her arms.

Gunnar rushed forward. The deputy hurried onto the porch and cuffed Kingston, hauling the man to his feet. "Jack, I'll take care of this," Gunnar said, sympathy all over his face. "And I'll get the ambulance out here for Caroline and Clarie."

"I'm fine," Caroline assured him, and she thought that might be true. Kingston had cut her, but it wasn't serious. Even if it had been, she probably wouldn't have admitted it. Not now. For now, she needed to hold Jack and get him through this.

"Kingston killed him," Jack muttered. "He killed him. And he tried to do the same to you."

"He failed," she reminded him, and she eased back so he could see her face. Her eyes. She wanted him to know that she was okay.

Jack shook his head like a man coming out of a trance, and his attention landed on her arm, then the side of her head. Where he no doubt saw blood.

"You need the EMTs," he insisted.

He snatched up his gun, holstering it, before he jumped down off the porch, pulling her down and into his arms. But he didn't stand her on the ground. Jack started carrying her toward the front of the inn.

"I can walk," she said.

However, she didn't fight him on this. It was something Jack needed, and she soon realized she needed it, too. She dropped her head onto his shoulder and let him soothe her in a way that only Jack could. Yes, there were still plenty of things unresolved, but she took these moments of comfort from him.

When they reached the front of the inn, she was thankful to see Clarie up and moving around. Manuel had brought in the other cruiser, and that was where Gunnar headed with Kingston. Clarie was rubbing her head and pacing in front of the other cruiser while she talked to someone on the phone.

"Don't worry, I'll let the EMTs check me out," Clarie immediately told Jack. "I just wanted to fill in Kellan. He'll meet us at the sheriff's office."

Caroline was exhausted, but she knew the night wasn't over, and she wanted to be there when Kellan booked Kingston. Actually, she wanted to be there for Jack and his brothers.

In the distance, Caroline heard the wail of sirens from the ambulance. But she also heard something else.

A shout.

"You bastard," someone yelled.

Jack immediately stood Caroline on the ground so he could pivot and draw his gun. But he was too late. The shot blasted through the air.

It took a moment for Caroline to fight through the shock and see what had happened. And then she spotted Grace. The woman was on the side of the front porch, a gun gripped in her hand.

A gun she'd just used to fire the shot.

At Kingston.

Grace hadn't missed, either. The shot had gone straight into Kingston's chest.

"You bastard," Grace repeated, the tears streaming down her face. She dropped her gun, and it clattered onto the porch. "That was for Scotty," she said before she lifted her hands in surrender.

Chapter Seventeen

Jack wasn't sure if it was a good sign that he did not feel anything but relief that Kingston was dead. As a lawman, he knew it would be a more fitting punishment for a killer to live out his life in a cage. But because there'd been the possibility of a mental facility rather than a prison, Jack was having a hard time seeing the man's death as a bad thing.

What was bad was that Grace would have to pay for what she had done. She might be spending the rest of her life in prison, and while that did bother him, Jack knew there'd been nothing he could have done to stop it. He hadn't seen Grace in time because he'd been so focused on getting help for Caroline and Clarie. Still, he wished he could have done something.

"Mentally beating yourself up?" Caroline asked.

Jack stopped his pacing so he could look at her. She was still on the treatment table in the

ER while a nurse finished up the three stitches she'd needed for her head. Four more stitches had already been put on her arm. Jack knew the nurse, Mary Ann Colley, and knew she was good at her job. She'd even stitched him up a few times.

Caroline's injuries were minor, he reminded himself, but Jack knew there was nothing minor when it came to Caroline. For the rest of his life, he'd see Kingston cutting her, and that was yet another reason he wasn't sorry the man was dead.

He nodded in response to her question, causing her to frown. Probably because she didn't believe beating himself up was necessary. But it was. He should have done a better job protecting her.

They'd gotten lucky. Not just with Caroline's injuries but with Clarie's, too. The deputy had also needed stitches and had a concussion, but she was going to make a full recovery and would only end up missing a couple days of work.

It could've been a lot worse. And not just with the injuries. Grace could have hit someone else when she'd been aiming at Kingston. Gunnar had been right there, but thankfully Grace's shot had hit only her intended target.

"Are you okay?" Caroline asked. She reached out, caught his hand and gave it a squeeze.

He knew what she was asking. This wasn't about the injuries now, or the aftermath of dealing with the attack. She wanted to know if Kingston's confession was eating a hole in him. In some ways, it was. The grief was right there at the surface. As fresh as it had been a year ago. But there was another side to this particular coin.

"I needed to know the truth," he settled for saying. "It's the start to dealing with this."

Caroline nodded, and he hated when he saw the tears she was blinking back. She quickly swiped one of them away. "Eric claimed a lot of lives," she whispered. "Kingston's included."

Jack huffed. "Now who's doing some mental beating up?" He got right in her face despite the fact that the nurse was there next to him. "I won't let you blame yourself for anything Eric did. And as for Kingston, he had a choice. He didn't have to do anything for Eric. Kingston did it because he wanted to do it. Hell, he took pleasure in it."

No way could she argue with that. Caroline had been there, with Kingston's knife to her throat, when the man had gloated and bragged. He likely would have turned into a killer even without Eric.

"All done," the nurse finally said. She stepped back from Caroline and took her hand to help her off the table. The woman handed Jack a piece of paper. "That's a script for some pain meds in case she needs it. The pharmacy's closed for the night, but if you give them a call, they'll open for you." She patted his arm. "Take good care of her, Jack. Give her lots of TLC."

Mary Ann added a wink, which meant she probably knew that Caroline and he had started up their relationship again. Heck, everybody in town probably knew. Jack frowned at that, not because of folks knowing, but because he wasn't sure exactly what his relationship was with Caroline.

He loved her, yes, and heck, they'd had sex twice since she'd gotten her memory back, but there hadn't been time to talk of the future and such. No time to do anything except try to hunt down a killer. With that done, Jack figured it was time for Caroline and him to have a long talk.

A talk that would apparently have to wait.

Jack realized that when he led Caroline out of the treatment room and spotted his brothers. All three of them. And they weren't alone. They had their fiancées, significant others and kids with them, too. On the surface, it looked to be an impromptu family reunion, but they were all there to try to deal with the grief of losing a father.

His brother Owen stood from one of the seats where he'd been sitting with his fiancée, Laney. She was holding Owen's toddler daughter, Addie, who was sacked out and totally unaware of the storm they'd all just weathered.

Eli stood with his girlfriend, Ashlyn. He was holding Ashlyn's adopted daughter, Cora. Cora was only a few months old and seemed entertained by all the people milling around.

Kellan was there with Gemma, and it was Gemma who came forward first and pulled Caroline into a gentle hug. She, too, was blinking back tears, and Jack figured Gemma was remembering her own nightmarish past with Eric, when he'd tried to kill her.

"I'm all right," Caroline assured her. Jack didn't know how she managed it, but Caroline even added a smile. One that looked surprisingly genuine.

"Caroline stood up to Kingston," Jack told Gemma. It wasn't pride in his voice. Okay, maybe it was a little of that, but it was mostly relief. It would likely make Caroline feel stronger now that she had done that. She hadn't been a victim tonight.

"I heard." Gemma glanced down at his raw knuckles. "And I heard you got in some punches. Good," she added before Jack could say anything. "I wish we could have all punched him a time or two."

So did Jack, because it had indeed helped to take out some of his grief and pain on his father's killer.

When Gemma stepped to the side, the others swarmed in. There were more hugs, more whispered words of comfort. His brothers and he all shared that silent conversation. A pact and a promise that they would get past this and get on with their lives.

Exactly what their father would have wanted them to do.

"Gunnar took Clarie home about ten minutes ago," Kellan explained. "She's fine, but I wanted her to get some rest."

That sounded like a darn good idea to Jack. He wanted the same for Caroline. "I'll need a vehicle." That was because Caroline and he had come to the hospital in an ambulance.

Kellan nodded. "Figured as much. You'll be taking Caroline to your house?" But Kellan waved that off. "Of course, you will be," his brother added at the same moment Caroline said, "Yes."

Jack looked at her to see if she had any doubts about that. Apparently, she didn't, since she brushed a kiss on his mouth. "Yes," she repeated.

Fighting a smile, Kellan took a key from his pocket. "Take my truck. Gemma and I can get home in one of the cruisers."

Jack thanked him and took the key. On the way to his place, he'd call the pharmacy and get those meds for Caroline. She didn't seem to be hurting, but that might not last. He fully intended to give her the meds and that TLC.

"The San Antonio cops have picked up Lily," Kellan continued a moment later. "The CSIs are going through Kingston's office. They've already found some things. Doctored files and such. She'll be charged with multiple felonies."

Jack knew he should probably care a whole lot more about that, and later he would. He wanted the woman punished for anything wrong she'd done. But for now, he had enough issues to deal with. And speaking of dealing, one of his current issues came through the door and into the hospital waiting room.

Zeller.

Hell. Jack hoped this didn't turn into a big blowup. Caroline didn't need that, and he wanted to get her out of there so she could rest. Apparently, his family had the same idea, because they, too, started to file out. All except Kellan. His brother stayed back, maybe be-

cause he thought there'd be some trouble between Zeller and him. If it was left up to Jack,
there wouldn't be.

Jack went to Zeller and met him eye to eye.
"I'm sorry," Jack told him.

Zeller opened his mouth. Clearly, the man
had geared up for some kind of argument, but
then he groaned softly and shook his head. "Everything was pointing to me. I looked guilty."

"Yeah, because Kingston paid Scotty to set
you up." Jack didn't point out that if Kingston
hadn't confessed, there might still be a dirty
smear on Zeller's reputation. Or at least the
questions and gossip.

"How's Grace?" Zeller asked.

Before Jack could answer, Caroline came
to his side and slid her arm around his waist.
Showing her support, no doubt. Jack appreciated it. Heck, he needed it, but he didn't like
that Caroline was going to have to listen to what
would likely turn into a chat about the wrap-up
of this investigation.

"Grace is in custody," Jack told him. "I'm
recommending a psych eval. Her mental state
definitely played into what she did tonight."

Ironic, since Kingston had been planning on
using that card for his own defense. In Grace's
case, though, it might be true. Still, even if she
went to prison for the rest of her life, it had been

her choice to pull the trigger. That was something Jack needed to remember.

Zeller nodded. "Good, but don't hold it against me if I say I'm glad that Kingston is dead. He tried to set me up. And he nearly succeeded."

Yeah, he had, and Jack figured there were a lot of people who wouldn't be mourning Kingston's death.

When Zeller stepped away to talk to Kellan, Jack knew that was his cue to get Caroline out of there. Unfortunately, the rain hadn't stopped. It was no longer coming down in buckets, but it was still drizzling.

"Wait here," he told her. "I'll bring Kellan's truck up to the door."

She glanced out the glass doors before turning to him and catching on to his hand. "We can walk. The fresh air and rain will feel good."

No, it probably wouldn't. It would just get them wet—again. But Jack really didn't care. The only thing that mattered right now was that Caroline was safe. And that she wanted him.

He had no trouble figuring that out when she leaned in and kissed him. Long and hard. Just the way he liked his kisses from Caroline. Of course, it stirred the heat. Always did, and when she finally eased back, they were both smiling.

And clearly eager to get home.

Jack grabbed a newspaper from a rack by the door, and he used that to cover their heads as they walked out. Not a mad dash but a slow stroll with Caroline's uninjured arm around his waist. They stopped long enough for another kiss. Then, another. By the time Jack finally got them in Kellan's truck, it felt as if they'd just gone through a round of foreplay. Foreplay that continued when Caroline dragged him back to her.

After he got his eyes uncrossed from the intense heat of it, he winked at her. "Are you just trying to get in my pants?"

"I've been in your pants. It's a nice place to be. In fact, I can say that your pants are the only ones I'll ever want to get into again."

Jack had been about to start the truck, but that stopped him so he could look at her. And kiss her again. "That means you'll have to marry me," he said.

She shook her head. "We don't have to be married for that."

He looked at her, making sure she saw that her answer would mean everything to him. *Everything*.

"Marry me," he insisted. "And don't make me repeat that whole outburst about me loving you more than I've ever loved anything or anybody."

"What if I want it repeated? What if I say it to you this time?" Caroline added before he could speak.

The corner of his mouth lifted, and he could have sworn his heart doubled in size. "I think I'd really like to hear that," he said.

She didn't take her eyes off him. "Believe me when I tell you that I love you. More than anybody else. More than anything. More than I ever thought it possible to love someone. Believe me when I tell you I'll marry you and that I'll spend the rest of my life showing you just how much I love you."

Smiling, Jack kissed her, his words whispering over her lips. "I believe you."

* * * * *

Look for more books by USA TODAY *bestselling author Delores Fossen from both Harlequin Intrigue and HQN Books coming soon!*

And don't miss the previous books in the Longview Ridge miniseries:

Safety Breach
A Threat to His Family
Settling an Old Score

Available now wherever Harlequin Intrigue books are sold!

Get 4 FREE REWARDS!

We'll send you 2 FREE Books plus 2 FREE Mystery Gifts.

Harlequin Romantic Suspense books are heart-racing page-turners with unexpected plot twists and irresistible chemistry that will keep you guessing to the very end.

FREE Value Over $20

YES! Please send me 2 FREE Harlequin Romantic Suspense novels and my 2 FREE gifts (gifts are worth about $10 retail). After receiving them, if I don't wish to receive any more books, I can return the shipping statement marked "cancel." If I don't cancel, I will receive 4 brand-new novels every month and be billed just $4.99 per book in the U.S. or $5.74 per book in Canada. That's a savings of at least 13% off the cover price! It's quite a bargain! Shipping and handling is just 50¢ per book in the U.S. and $1.25 per book in Canada.* I understand that accepting the 2 free books and gifts places me under no obligation to buy anything. I can always return a shipment and cancel at any time. The free books and gifts are mine to keep no matter what I decide.

240/340 HDN GNMZ

Name (please print)

Address   Apt. #

City   State/Province   Zip/Postal Code

Email: Please check this box ☐ if you would like to receive newsletters and promotional emails from Harlequin Enterprises ULC and its affiliates. You can unsubscribe anytime.

Mail to the **Reader Service:**
IN U.S.A.: P.O. Box 1341, Buffalo, NY 14240-8531
IN CANADA: P.O. Box 603, Fort Erie, Ontario L2A 5X3

Want to try 2 free books from another series! Call 1-800-873-8635 or visit www.ReaderService.com.

Get 4 FREE REWARDS!

We'll send you 2 FREE Books plus 2 FREE Mystery Gifts.

Harlequin Presents books feature the glamorous lives of royals and billionaires in a world of exotic locations, where passion knows no bounds.

FREE
Value Over
$20

Get 4 FREE REWARDS!

We'll send you 2 FREE Books plus 2 FREE Mystery Gifts.

FREE
Value Over
$20

Both the **Romance** and **Suspense** collections feature compelling novels written by many of today's bestselling authors.

YES! Please send me 2 FREE novels from the Essential Romance or Essential Suspense Collection and my 2 FREE gifts (gifts are worth about $10 retail). After receiving them, if I don't wish to receive any more books, I can return the shipping statement marked "cancel." If I don't cancel, I will receive 4 brand-new novels every month and be billed just $7.24 each in the U.S. or $7.49 each in Canada. That's a savings of up to 28% off the cover price. It's quite a bargain! Shipping and handling is just 50¢ per book in the U.S. and $1.25 per book in Canada.* I understand that accepting the 2 free books and gifts places me under no obligation to buy anything. I can always return a shipment and cancel at any time. The free books and gifts are mine to keep no matter what I decide.

Choose one: ☐ **Essential Romance**
(194/394 MDN GQ6M)   ☐ **Essential Suspense**
(191/391 MDN GQ6M)

Name (please print)

Address   Apt. #

City   State/Province   Zip/Postal Code

Email: Please check this box ☐ if you would like to receive newsletters and promotional emails from Harlequin Enterprises ULC and its affiliates. You can unsubscribe anytime.

Mail to the **Reader Service:**
IN U.S.A.: P.O. Box 1341, Buffalo, NY 14240-8531
IN CANADA: P.O. Box 603, Fort Erie, Ontario L2A 5X3

Want to try 2 free books from another series! Call **1-800-873-8635** or visit www.ReaderService.com.

---

*Terms and prices subject to change without notice. Prices do not include sales taxes, which will be charged (if applicable) based on your state or country of residence. Canadian residents will be charged applicable taxes. Offer not valid in Quebec. This offer is limited to one order per household. Books received may not be as shown. Not valid for current subscribers to the Essential Romance or Essential Suspense Collection. All orders subject to approval. Credit or debit balances in a customer's account(s) may be offset by any other outstanding balance owed by or to the customer. Please allow 4 to 6 weeks for delivery. Offer available while quantities last.

Your Privacy—Your information is being collected by Harlequin Enterprises ULC, operating as Reader Service. For a complete summary of the information we collect, how we use this information and to whom it is disclosed, please visit your privacy notice located at corporate.harlequin.com/privacy-notice. From time to time we may also exchange your personal information with reputable third parties. If you wish to opt out of this sharing of your personal information, please visit readerservice.com/consumerschoice or call 1-800-873-8635. **Notice to California Residents**—Under California law, you have specific rights to control and access your data. For more information on these rights and how to exercise them, visit corporate.harlequin.com/california-privacy.

STRS20R2

THE WESTERN HEARTS COLLECTION!

19 FREE BOOKS in all!

COWBOYS. RANCHERS. RODEO REBELS.
Here are their charming love stories in one prized Collection:
51 emotional and heart-filled romances that capture the majesty and rugged beauty of the American West!

YES! Please send me **The Western Hearts Collection** in Larger Print. This collection begins with 3 FREE books and 2 FREE gifts in the first shipment. Along with my 3 free books, I'll also get the next 4 books from The Western Hearts Collection, in LARGER PRINT, which I may either return and owe nothing, or keep for the low price of $5.45 U.S./$6.23 CDN each plus $2.99 U.S./$7.49 CDN for shipping and handling per shipment*. If I decide to continue, about once a month for 8 months I will get 6 or 7 more books but will only need to pay for 4. That means 2 or 3 books in every shipment will be FREE! If I decide to keep the entire collection, I'll have paid for only 32 books because 19 books are FREE! I understand that accepting the 3 free books and gifts places me under no obligation to buy anything. I can always return a shipment and cancel at any time. My free books and gifts are mine to keep no matter what I decide.

☐ 270 HCN 5354   ☐ 470 HCN 5354

Name (please print)

Address   Apt. #

City   State/Province   Zip/Postal Code

Mail to the **Reader Service:**
IN U.S.A.: P.O. Box 1341, Buffalo, N.Y. 14240-8531
IN CANADA: P.O. Box 603, Fort Erie, Ontario L2A 5X3